And The Goat Cried

Henry A. Buchanan

AND THE GOAT CRIED

❧ ❧ ❧

Southern Tales
And Other
Chance Meetings

CREATIVE ARTS BOOK COMPANY
Berkeley • 1998

And The Goat Cried is published by Donald S. Ellis and
distributed by Creative Arts Book Company.

For Information contact:
Creative Arts Book Company
833 Bancroft Way
Berkeley, California 94710

ISBN 0-88739-115-X
Library of Congress Catalog Number 97-66001

Printed in the United States of America

DEDICATION

And The Goat Cried is dedicated to all who find some
redeeming humor even in life's most common tragedies
and all who know that even life's brightest joys
are ever shadowed by hovering tragedy.

ACKNOWLEDGMENTS

I hereby acknowledge my debt to all the old curmudgeons at The Sunrise Café. And where shall I hide when they find themselves in this little collection of stories?!

TABLE OF CONTENTS

AUTHOR'S NOTE

Lacking the service of anyone I can rely on to say something both nice and true about my stories, I am writing my own preface.

The stories in this little book were not written in the vain hope of changing the world for the better, or even of painting a picture of the world as it ought to be. I have told these stories to describe the world as it was in the days of my boy hood, and even before; as it was in the years of my youth and young manhood, and as it is today. It was and is a black and white world with never enough gray matter to go around, but always with enough humor in it to have a redeeming influence on it. If you see yourself in my stories, dear reader, I hope you can laugh at yourself. That will make it easier for the rest of us to live with you.

Now go ahead. Enjoy! There will be more to follow for this little book has only dipped lightly from the spring where winged pegasus waters.

Henry A. Buchanan
Murray, Kentucky • 1997

And The Goat Cried

The Deaf Shall Be
Made To Hear

Uncle Jim and Aunt Lizzie lived on a fourteen acre farm near Albany Georgia in the years between the two great wars. Uncle Jim claimed he had married Aunt Lizzie in a fit of insanity and that by the time he had regained his senses it was too late. The house was full of younguns and he had to raise them.

Papa said Uncle Jim's mental aberration returned on special occasions and that one of those occasions coincided with Papa's annual visit. Aunt Lizzie was Papa's sister; this was the reason for his visit. What brought on the events which occurred while he was visiting his sister has to be chalked up to Uncle Jim's peculiarities though.

Uncle Jim was what is known as a practical joker. I have never seen anything practical about the kind of stunts Uncle Jim pulled and it is questionable whether they even qualify as jokes, but I will tell you what he did to Papa and you can call it what you want to. Uncle Jim had been looking forward to Papa's visit with high expectations of great pleasure at Papa's expense, and he had set the stage for the little drama which took place less than two hours after Papa's arrival.

"Jake Hennessey lives down the road a little piece," Uncle Jim told Papa. "He says he wants to meet you. I have told him you are Lizzie's brother and he says if you are anything like Lizzie it will he better than when the circus comes to town and sets up in the same tent with the holiness preacher."

Flattery will easily get you what you want with Papa. He agreed to go with Uncle Jim to meet Jake Hennessey because he had already caught up with the news of what had happened to his sister Lizzie since his last visit. He was eager to get out of the house. Uncle Jim said "We will go in my old Tin Lizzie." The Tin Lizzie was a Model T. Ford which Uncle Jim claimed he could "hold together forever with baling wire."

Jake Hennessey lived a couple of miles down the road from Uncle Jim. Papa climbed into the Ford and they rattled off down the road at a fast clip of about fifteen miles an hour. The road was like a washboard and Papa said "My God, Jim Tack, if you don't slow down you'll shake my false teeth out of my head."

Uncle Jim ignored this: remark; he had something else on his mind. "Now there's one thing I have to tell you about Jake before we get there," Uncle Jim said in a conspiratorial tone. "Jake's deaf as a fence post on the back side of the pasture. If you want him to hear what you've got to say you'll hafta speak up."

Papa had a strong voice anyway and under duress it would compare favorably with the bullhorn the county sheriff used when he was controlling the crowds that gathered at the scene of a fire. Uncle Jim thought about this and he reckoned that Papa would be able to reach Jake's understanding if he got up real close to him. "Stand close and speak into his right ear. I believe that's the one that's better than the other one."

They bumped along in the old flivver past cotton patches and corn fields without saying much more about Jake Hennessey.

Papa knew they had arrived when he saw the mail box. It had the name Hennessey painted on it in red letters that ran down at the feet and dripped onto the ground. The box clung to a leaning post and seemed ready to accept whatever personal correspondence and advertising circulars the rural mail carrier might bring on his daily rounds. The door to the mail box hung by one hinge; this saved the mail carrier the trouble of opening and closing it every day.

Uncle Jim shut off the engine to save gas and leaned over to Papa; he put his hand on Papa's knee cap to keep him from jumping out of the car. "Now you just set right here and rest up after your long trip down here and then having to listen to Lizzie recall her life history. I'll go to the door and fetch Jake. I'll try to make him understand who you are before I bring him out here to meet you. That will make it easier on everybody."

Once he was inside the house Uncle Jim held a little tete-a-tete with Jake. "My brother-in-law is out there in the car and I know you'll enjoy talking with him but first I need to tell you he's hard of hearing; he won't know a word you're saying to him unless you get up close enough to put it right in his ear. I believe his left ear is the one you oughtta use. And don't whisper neither."

Jake hitched up his overalls, cut a fresh plug of Brown's Mule with his pocket knife and said he felt equal to the task. He and Uncle Jim walked out to the car and Uncle Jim made the introductions in a voice that could have been heard eight miles away in Albany. Then the two, Papa and Jake set themselves to the job of breaking the sound barrier in order to exchange information, opinions and speculations about the future of the country in terms of the weather, crop conditions, breeding of cattle, prices of all these things and politics in general.

These subjects all came after the initial greeting though. Jake yelled for Papa to "get out and come in," standing as close to Papa as he could get, allowing for the wide running boards on Uncle Jim's Model "T" Ford. Papa was already in the act of jumping down from the front seat and he made a miss step, overshot the running board and fell upon Jake's neck like the father of the prodigal son in the Bible.

From this close position Papa was able to tell Jake how glad he was to meet him because of all the good things Jim Tack had told him. Jake, for his part, was able to hear what Papa said but seemed to be a bit concerned lest Papa bite his ear off in the process. Papa backed up what he'd said with some philosophy, or maybe it was theology; he said "God don't put a man on this earth without giving him some redeeming feature."

Jake didn't know what to make of this statement because he feared it might mean Papa was a religious fanatic, which he wasn't, although he had been baptized twice. The first time he was sprinkled a Methodist when he was just a boy. Then later he was put all the way under by the Baptists at Mount Zion. They wouldn't have him with just a dry cleaning so they gave him a real baptizing.

After Papa and Jake and Uncle Jim were all seated on the porch Jake dragged his chair over close to Papa and got into position to carry on a conversation. That's when all the talk about the weather and everything took place. "It's awful dry here in the county," Jake said. "Ain't had rain in more'n two weeks and there ain't enough water in the creek to wet the crawfishes' behinds."

Papa leaned close to Jake's right ear and shouted "Ain't never knowed it to come a good rain in the middle of a long dry spell."

These and other observations were delivered and received gladly by both of the deaf men who glanced now and then at Uncle Jim for verification that what was being said was also being heard. Uncle Jim watched the progress of this dialogue and after about forty minutes he decided to bring the shouting match to an end because it was obvious that both Papa and Jake were suffering from parched throat brought on by the unusual stress and strain on the vocal cords) he had a solution for the problem.

"I am a bit thirsty" he announced, "and I just remembered that I brought along a flask of the best moonshine made in this part of Georgia. I left it out in the car though, in that little side pocket on the door. Now I will have to go after it, but you two just go ahead with your visiting while I fetch the moonshine."

Uncle Jim said this in a normal conversational tone, maybe almost in a whisper, and both Papa and Jake were surprised to note that what Uncle Jim had said was evidently heard clearly by everybody concerned because both Papa and Jake responded properly and favorably to the suggestion without requiring Uncle Jim to repeat what he had said.

"I'll git some glasses from the kitchen," Jake said. "We'll just do it up right. Wisht I had some ice but the ice man don't come until tomorrow."

Papa said "We don't need no ice. Don't need to add nothing to good moonshine. When the good Lord made moonshine He done a perfect job."

Jake wondered again if Papa was a religious fanatic but he didn't make an issue of it. Everybody was more concerned about getting the moonshine in the glasses without spilling a drop of it than about who actually made the moonshine. They had finished off the first round and started in on the second when Papa was suddenly hit by a thunderbolt of understanding of what had happened to him.

"God A'mighty!" Papa said. "Jim Tack has done played a prank on both of us. Or else that moonshine is the best damn cure for deafness ever invented by humankind!"

Whose Hose Is Longest?

"I don't care what you need it for Oscar!" Ethel was angry. Her anger showed in the way she walked. Stamping the ground. In her voice. Strident. Her face. Flushed. "I am tired of having to track down the hose every time I want to water my garden. Now I've walked myself to death hunting for the hose, and YOU have it."

Ethel did not appear to be near death, but she gave every evidence of being able to inflict death on Oscar. And he knew he would lose this battle but he would not go down to ignominious defeat without making a heroic defense. "Yes, Water your damn' peas. You've got a dime's worth of peas at stake there and I've got five hundred dollars in trees that are dying because it won't rain." He left the impression that Ethel was somehow responsible for the lack of rain. "And you're..." He spluttered out at this point because he had been caught red handed with Ethel's garden hose. Or is it green handed when the hose is made of green vinyl?

Whatever the color of the hose, Oscar and Ethel were having a little domestic struggle over the garden hose which stretched from the hydrant on the side of the house to the ever thirsty tomatoes, peas, corn and...and...and yes, TREES. The TREES were the root of the trouble too. For Oscar had planted the trees in the garden area which Ethel had claimed as HER Garden Plot. That plot of ground was HER veggie and flower garden, a combination unusual if not unique as a result of Ethel's having read in one of her gardening magazines that certain flowers, marigolds for instance, protect the vegetables against bad insects, and others, Queen Anne's lace, attract good insects which pollinate the beans and tomatoes. And Oscar had planted

TREES in her garden plot!

Oh not exactly IN her garden plot. In fact, Oscar had planted the trees on the North border in what he termed an artistic pattern, a curving line that dipped down at the East and West ends but did not dare enter the territory of the corn and the squashes occupying those areas of Ethel's garden.

With her eyes fixed on those trees where the line dipped toward the garden, Ethel asked "Why couldn't you plant them on a straight line on the boundary line the way anybody else would have done?"

It always angered Oscar to be asked why he didn't do anything the way others do, but he restrained himself and said "God."

"God? !"

"Yes, God. He created the whole universe without a straight line in it. Who am I to spit in the Face of God by planting my trees in a straight line?"

"No chance of that!" Ethel thought how good it would be if God would commission Oscar to plant the planet Mars with trees all in a circle.

But there were Oscar's trees in a curving line on planet Earth. "Those trees are going to shade my garden and nothing will grow in the shade." She stared balefully at the artistically curving line of little white pine trees on the Northern border.

"Not unless the world tilts on its axis so dramatically that we'll all fall off with your squashes and cantaloupes falling on top of us." Oscar appeared smug in this knowledge of cosmic events and Ethel gave him that stare which means "Explain yourself if you're so smart!"

Oscar was proud to display his scientific acumen and he pointed out to Ethel a fact gleaned from a fifth grade science book, that trees always cast their shadows to the North, never to the South. "Except one day in the year, at the Summer Solstice when the shadow will be directly under the tree, then it will begin to..."

But Ethel stopped him from explaining the mystery in greater detail which he had fully intended to do. She said "The tree roots will take up all the nutrients in the soil and no matter how much fertilizer I put down those blasted tree roots will starve my peas and beans to death."

"Blasted" was about as near as Ethel dared to come to saying "damned" because this confrontation took place on Monday morning following the Sunday on which the Reverend Ebenezer Goodbody had spoken strongly against the use of profanity. Even Oscar had applauded the Reverend's efforts saying "a damned good sermon!" But Ethel's use of euphemisms did not lack any of the force of Oscar's more graphic profanity. Her new line of attack did cause Oscar to launch into another exegesis though, on roots and branches of trees.

"The roots extend out approximately the same distance as the branches and you can see that the branches of these little evergreens do not even come near your precious pea rows." Oscar's branch/root theory got short shrift from Ethel who declared that she had turned up tree roots in the middle of her garden.

"And they were all wrapped around the tines of my Troybilt tiller too." She could not produce the evidence to support this charge though and Oscar scoffed at it.

"Tommyrot" he snorted. "More likely the roots of those damned okra stalks you turned under last fall and they're still lying there waiting for you to wet them down so they can sprout again."

Wetting the okra stalks brought the discussion back to water and the use of the garden hose and the conflict between peas and trees. Ethel, in the interest of harmony said "They make a two pronged connection so you can attach two hoses and then two people can use the water at the same time." There was not enough hose for this experiment though, and Oscar drove to town to buy this new fangled gadget which would bring peace and harmony into the family. It gave him an opportunity to spend an hour at the Sunrise Cafe drinking-coffee with his old cronies.

"It will give Ethel time to cool off," he reasoned. And when he came back with the miracle peace maker gadget he had bought a hundred feet of hose to extend from it to his trees. But when he turned the water on at the hydrant the water flowed freely to the thirsty pine trees but nary a drop reached Ethel's Brussels Sprouts.

Close inspection revealed that the cut-off valves worked in a strange fashion. The one which opened for Oscar's side was pointed along the hose when open, but when Ethel's valve was

turned the same way it was closed. This conflict was finally ame-
liorated by careful adjustments resulting in a drastic reduction in
the flow of water to both the trees and the vegetables because
there was not enough pressure to feed both lines at once.

"I will just have to hook my hose to another hydrant," Oscar
concluded. This called for more hose which meant making
another trip to the farm store, and more coffee at the Sunrise.
Oscar came back this time with two hundred feet of hose and
Ethel promptly appropriated half of it because the coupling on
her hose was leaking and wasting water.

By this time the day was well spent and Oscar realized that he
was due at his Book Club meeting where he was committed to
lead the discussion on Eric Hoffer's THE TRUE BELIEVER dealing with fanaticism and mass movements. As he rushed off to
the meeting he called back to Ethel "Shut off the water for me,
will you Ethel?"

Ethel nodded her consent and went on watering her garden.
When she was finished she shut off the water to her veggies and
flowers but she did not give Oscar's trees a thought. It was late
when Oscar came home and he only asked "Did you think to
shut off the water?" Because by now he was beginning to think
about the water bill which he had already reminded Ethel would
be greater than that of the Persian Gulf War. Ethel said "Yes" to
his inquiry and went on reading from the latest issue of Organic
Gardening Made Easy.

Next morning Oscar went out to turn the water on his pine
trees again and he found that one of them, the one on which he
had left the hose the evening before, had floated out of the
ground and the water was still flowing into the pool which had
formed where the tree had been.

"OMIGOD!" Oscar wept.

Drunk Again

Jake Bethune was nineteen years old. Dark of hair and complexion. Black, pig eyes. Heavy set and muscular. Strong as a bull. Obstinate as a mule, quick tempered too.

Jake had a problem. Drinking. To state the matter another way: Jake WAS a problem to his mother, because of his drinking.

Hattie Belle Bethune, Jake's mother, was a saintly woman. A woman of deep religious convictions. Deepest of all her religious convictions was the belief that unless her son Jake stopped getting drunk, a terrible thing was going to happen when he died; he was going to hell. And getting drunk was going to hasten his demise and consequent descent into the nether regions.

Because Hattie Belle feared that her son Jake would die—quite possibly die a violent death—and go to hell because of his drunken behavior, she sought the solace and help of her minister, Brother Clarence Ogilvie.

Brother Ogilvie, a Baptist preacher known to be a hard line teetotaler and an outspoken enemy of John Barleycorn, received Sister Hattie Belle with a great outpouring of sympathy and verbal assurances that both he and the Lord understood her problem and much desired the salvation of her son Jake.

Clarence Ogilvie was about fifty years old, balding, ruddy of complexion and noticeably overweight. Gluttony, he conceded, was a sin but not in the same class with drunkenness.

Brother Ogilvie had a powerful pulpit voice and he never apologized for its loudness, for he felt that he was always witnessing for the Lord, whether it was to a congregation of many or an audience of one. "Sit down, Sister Hattie Belle," Brother Ogilvie thundered, his voice reverberating and bouncing off the wall of his tiny study room directly behind the baptistry which was directly behind the pulpit of the Friendship Baptist Church. "You have come about your boy Jake I presume."

He had presumed correctly. Hattie Belle Bethune pushed a strand of grey hair from her watery blue eyes; she worked her toothless gums and swallowed; her Adam's Apple bobbed as she tried to compose her wrinkled face. "I have come about my boy Jake," she repeated the preacher's words. "And I pray God you can help me."

Brother Ogilvie thought it might be more effective if Hattie Belle prayed that God Himself would intervene, for his own efforts on young Jake's behalf had been ineffective. But he nodded his head encouragingly to her.

"I am at the end of my rope, Brother Ogilvie." Hattie Belle spoke in a breaking voice. "Jake is the child of my old age. I was past forty when he was born and I thought my childbearing days were over. But then there he was inside me, and I have done my best for him since he come into this world. His Daddy died five years ago and now I am left to carry the burden alone in my old age." She shifted uncomfortably on the straight back chair. "My burden is a heavy one, Brother Ogilvie."

"It IS a heavy burden, sister," the preacher said. "But the Lord will not lay more on us than we can bear."

Hattie Belle was set back momentarily by this reply, even though she had heard it all of her life; she was not to be put off so easily though. "Then the Lord did not lay it upon me, but he will have to help me bear it if I am to hold up much longer."

Warming to the contest, she recounted her efforts on her wayward son's behalf. "I have begged and pleaded with him. On bended knee. I have read to him from the Bible and I have prayed for his immortal soul. I have even had Hansford Cherry to come over and talk with him. Hansford is a member of the AA and he tells me he has not touched a drop in six months."

Hansford Cherry's six months record of sobriety met with Brother Ogilvie's approval but he would rather give the Lord the credit rather than Alcoholics Anonymous. Brother Ogilvie thought that six months was about as long as Hansford Cherry would make it without the Lord's supporting arms.

Hattie Belle continued her account. "I have talked to Jake's boss at the feed mill. And Ellwood Spottsworthy is a good man and he wants Jake to do right. But Ellwood is known to get high himself now and then, and I guess it is a matter of the pot calling the kettle black for him to talk to Jake."

Brother Ogilvie nodded his head vigorously at this remark and Hattie Belle added "He says as long as Jake shows up for work sober on Monday morning there ain't a thing he can do about it." Brother Ogilvie started to nod again , then shook his head despairingly at the mention of Ellwood Spottsworthy's weakness for the bottle.

"And now Jake has got that big old car and he goes racing all over in it and I'm scared he will kill himself. If somebody else don't kill him. You know how he gets into fights when he's drunk."

"What does Jake say when you talk to him about his drinking, Sister Hattie Belle?" Brother Ogilvie had heard all of this before and he had run out of suggestions, and was even running short on pious platitudes for getting Jake to straighten up and walk the chalk line.

"Oh he is always contrite when he sobers up. Says he will never touch it again. But then he's back out there at Big Eddie Taylor's where he knows he can get that old moon shine even if the liquor stores won't sell him the legal stuff because they know him."

Brother Ogilvie was getting restless because the problem would not go away, so he said "Sister Hattie Belle, let us go to the Lord in prayer and lay this burden of Jake's sin before the throne of Grace. We'll just ask the Lord to help."

Hattie Belle's eyes brightened for a moment at the prospect of prayer offered by this man of God, but hope was soon dimmed by memory, for even Brother Ogilvie had prayed for Jake before. Yet she bowed her grey head and folded her gnarled hands in her lap and Brother Ogilvie prayed.

"Oh Lord we beseech Thee on Jake's behalf. Turn him from paths of destruction and cause him to walk in the paths of righteousness and sobriety."

With many more words of supplication Brother Ogilvie sought Divine intervention, and when his prayer was ended Hattie Belle Bethune, who had fallen to her knees while the preacher prayed, rose stiffly and painfully and extended her hand in gratitude, and for help in getting to her feet.

"Surely the Lord will hear that prayer for you are a good man

Brother Ogilvie. Surely this time the Lord will intervene and save my boy."

"The Lord works in mysterious ways..." Brother Ogilvie intoned, and Hattie Belle caught upon that promise.

"It is Saturday, Brother Ogilvie. If my boy comes home sober tonight it will be the first Saturday night in over a year. Pray, oh pray that he will!"

Hattie Belle, muttering more prayers under her breath, turned and walked back to her little house which was no more than two blocks from the Friendship Baptist Church.

It was late afternoon and she began preparing the evening meal and watching the clock. For she knew that Jake would get off work at four thirty. The whistle blew at the Feed Mill and she hastened to put the food on the table, checking to be sure that everything would be piping hot.

The clock on the mantle struck five, then five thirty, then six, but Jake had not come home. Then she heard a car door slam outside and she smiled deep inside herself, praising God and turning anxiously, expectantly, to watch the door. The door opened, but it was not Jake.

It was Jesse, Jake's older brother. Disappointment shoved on her face, and Jesse said "What's the matter Ma? You don't look glad to see me."

"Oh, I'm glad to see you Son but I hoped it was Jake." Jesse stood there looking at her and she burst into tears.

"Maybe I oughtta go," he said, for he had no patience with his younger brother, but his mother clung to him and would not let him go.

"Stay and eat," she pleaded. "I reckon he ain't coming." So Jesse stayed and he ate sparingly for he knew that his wife would expect him to eat at home. Besides, he had no appetite for the food prepared for his younger brother. Hattie Belle picked at the food too, and finally she gave it up. After a while Jesse pushed his chair back from the table.

"I better get on home. Elaine and the kids will he looking for me. I don't want them to think I'm out somewhere drunk." He knew this would hurt his mother as well as he knew Elaine would not think he was drunk because he had never been, but he had to say it because of the way he felt toward his younger brother, so he took his hat and got into the car and drove away and Hattie Belle stood in the door watching as he turned the corner onto the next street.

Then she went back to wait and watch and listen to the striking of the clock but Jake didn't come and he didn't come and he didn't come. And on the stroke of twelve midnight she stood in the open doorway watching. Car lights appeared on the street and the big Buick whirled into the driveway and came to a skidding halt near the front steps. It was Jake.

Jake pulled himself to his feet, muttering and mumbling unintelligibly. He left the car door swinging open and seemed to be taking his bearings on the front door. Or on the figure standing in the doorway. With staggering steps he made it across the short space between the car and the steps leading up to the porch on the front of the house. He stumbled twice on the steps. Cursing and regaining his footing at last he made it to the porch where he swayed to and fro, trying to focus on the frail figure standing not more than five feet from him. She was gripping the door facing so hard that her swollen knuckles hurt.

Then in a voice of utter hopelessness tinged with disgust, that frail figure in the doorway opened her mouth and spoke two words.

"Drunk Again!"

And Jake swayed on his feet, lurched forward into her arms and said "Yeah. Me too, Ma. Me too."

Yesterday's Toast

Oscar Bayberry awakened in a foul mood on that Tuesday in June when everything that could go wrong actually went berserk. This presaged a bad day for Oscar and for others who might come into contact with him. It is possible that Oscar himself could foresee it but the others were probably taken by surprise.

Truth to tell Oscar was not allowed to awaken and that was where it all began. He was waked up by Ethel who had awakened because she had an inner clock which went off in her brain, reminding her that she had many things to do in the garden today. Things which would require Oscar's help. "Cooperation" is the term commonly used for such joint endeavors as digging post holes and stringing wire fence. That euphonious term did not fit on Oscar's tongue. "Slave labor" Oscar called it. "When Ethel sees me heading for my desk she intercepts me with some job that has to be done in that damned garden."

Oscar had planned to spend the day at his desk, writing. He saw himself as a writer of stories some true, some made up. Ethel had gardening on her brain. "Wake up Oscar!" Ethel called out as she shook the sleeping form on the bed. "I want you to help me in the garden but we have to go to the Co-op first to get a few things." She started to tell him all the things she needed and what she needed each one of them for and why she failed to get them the last time she was in town.

"Ethel always has a dozen things to do before she can start on what she has set out to do." Oscar was wont to grumble. "And all thirteen of them involve me!" Oscar rose grumpily from his sleep, sat on the edge of the bed for a minute, getting his bearings on the world which continued to spin in its orbit in spite of his grumpiness, rose painfully to his feet because now the pressure on his bladder was more insistent than the need for sleep.

They were off to the farm store before breakfast because Ethel wanted to be there when the store opened. "At six, I believe, in the busy gardening season. I don't like to have to wait in line while every farmer in the county is gathering up his supplies for the whole year's work." They got to the farm store at six twenty five because Oscar dragged around and Ethel found that she had to clip some flower heads that were beginning to fade. A sign on the door indicated a seven o'clock opening. Even at seven some of the workers at the farm store arrived before they were fully awake and ready to do business. As a consequence of this, some difficulty arose over the order that Ethel gave for fencing for her cucumber vines to climb on in spite of the fact that she explained to the boy who was waiting on her that the cucumbers were already coming up and needed something to climb on and they would be running all over the ground if she didn't get the fence up for them to climb.

"I told the boy five foot fencing and six foot posts," she explained defensively to Oscar later when they had got home and had started to erect the fence. "How did I know the silly thing was going to give me six foot fencing and five foot posts?"

That was only part of the mixup. When Oscar and Ethel got to the car with the wire fencing and the posts protruding from the luggage compartment Ethel said to Oscar, "Did the boy give you the clips?"

"Why would the boy give me clips?" Oscar was puzzled.

"He said they would furnish enough clips to fasten the fencing to the posts. Free." Ethel was not one to pass up freebies although Oscar protested that he had already bought a package of clips and it was only a matter of finding them somewhere in the garage.

Ethel thought that finding anything Oscar had put away would be like finding the pot of gold at the end of a rainbow. She sent him back to the desk to get the clips. "That will be a dollar fifty nine for a package of clips," the clerk at the counter told Oscar.

"I thought the clips went with the posts."

"They do. How many posts do you want?"

"I don't WANT posts. My wife has already bought the posts."

"I have to charge you for the clips if you're not buying posts."

"My wife has already paid for the posts."

"How many posts?"

"What damned difference does it make? They're bought, paid for and loaded in the car. Do I get the clips or not?"

"Sir, I have to tell the boy how many clips to count out and for that I have to know how many posts you bought. Or, as you claim, your wife bought. Otherwise I have to charge you for the clips."

That was the trip to the farm store. When Oscar had unloaded the posts, the fencing and the clips - twelve, count them, four for each post - he remembered that he had not had any breakfast. He thought of a bowl of cereal but he could not be seen going toward the house. Too risky. Ethel would find another little job for him. He got into the car and drove to town and entered the Sunrise Cafe where he was accustomed to meeting his old cronies for coffee, a gab feet and a sharing of complaints. Nobody was there. He was puzzled and thought maybe he was too early but after about five minutes the waitress came and he said to her "Where is everybody?" "They've gone," she said. "You're late."

"Bring me coffee and toast." Oscar was surprised to discover that he was actually disappointed. "Why," he said under his breath, "I believe I actually miss the old bastards." Then he noticed that time passes slowly when you sit down alone in a restaurant. "No," he thought. "Time does not pass. It drags sluggishly." In about ten minutes - his estimate, he failed to check his watch - she brought the coffee.

"Where's the toast?" he asked. "I ordered toast too."

"I told him. He's fixing it." She didn't say who "he" was. Oscar assumed that "he" was a faceless, or invisible cook.

The waitress set the coffee down on the table while looking off at the people at the next table. There were four of them. They were jovial and seeming to have a great old time. She went and stood by the table, order pad in hand, writing down the order which was given her between loud bursts of laughter.

Oscar sipped his coffee. He thought "No toast." He sipped again. Still no toast. Finally he gulped the coffee. It was no long hot. He drained the cup and let it clatter on the table. He thoug "She will come back to refill my cup and maybe she will br the toast then."

She didn't come back to refill his coffee cup. He picked it up and twirled it around in his hand, examined it, found it just as empty as it was before. Set it on the table again. Let it clatter a bit louder this time. He waited, watching the waitress move from table to table and from table to kitchen and back to tables but she did not look in his direction . "So!" he thought. "No toast. No coffee refill."

After fifteen minutes -estimated - he got up and left a nickel tip on the table. He went to the cash register to pay for the coffee. She was there. "Don't you want your toast?"

"I did. Not now. I've changed my mind."

"He's making it now. If you want it, it'll be ready in a minute."

"I don't want it now."

"You don't have to take it just because you ordered it but it's there if you want it. He's fixing it now."

"I've changed my mind. I don't want it now."

Oscar left. He was disgruntled. It had been a bad day. Even if he went back to his desk now, the muse would not sit on his shoulder. Only his poison pen would have ink in it. Chalk it up for a lost day. Tomorrow would be a better day. Oscar was an optimist for the moment. How could tomorrow be worse?

Tomorrow came, bringing with it the realization that he had acted like a horse's ass at the farm store and a nincompoop at the Sunrise Cafe. But even in his most penitent moods a man must have coffee; it goes with wearing sack cloth and with ashes on his head. Oscar walked into the Sunrise. All of his old cronies were there, gathered about their favorite table by the North wall. They were in a pleasant mood. They looked up and welcomed Oscar. The waitress came smiling, coffee in hand. Toast too.

"Now this is service" Oscar said, as the old bastards all looked on in surprise, thinking: How does he rate this?

"Oh!" she said, "The toast. Yes. It's been ready ever since yesterday. See? I saved it for you!"

My Son The Lawyer

Caleb Ledbetter was an old Kentucky ridge runner. He grew tobacco - about three acres of it - on the ridge which ran along the top of his eighty acre farm like the backbone of a dinosaur.

At one time, before they went to the poundage system, the government told Caleb how many acres of tobacco he could grow. That was called his tobacco base. If he planted more than his allotted acreage, when the government man came to measure it, Caleb had to cut down the excess or the government would jerk the floor out from under him, which means that he would lose the price support that enabled him to operate at a profit, or he wouldn't be allowed to sell his tobacco, or maybe some worse fate would befall him because when a plain dirt farmer gets in trouble with the federal government, then he is up to his fetlocks in the worst kind of trouble. To be hauled into court by the government is the next thing to facing the executioner's axe.

So Caleb was greatly encouraged when his only son Jim Henry announced that he was going to study to become a lawyer because if a man has his own lawyer right in the family he is one up and a jump ahead of anybody else in the race.

Jim Henry was a bright boy and he was accepted by the Law School at Lexington and when he had been attending for about a year Caleb said to his wife Mattie Belle "Now that boy is as smart as any Philadelphia lawyer and I will just get him to help me out with this matter with the county road department."

Caleb's trouble with the road department came about because of a downpour of rain that brought Stony Fork Creek raging out of its banks. The flooding of Stony Fork washed out a bridge and damaged the foundation of an old tobacco barn downstream.

But opportunity presents itself with many faces and the county judge applied for a federal grant for flood control measures and in his eagerness to spend the million dollars the government granted he got together with the superintendent of roads to determine how they could best spend the federal dollars to produce the most votes. They sent a bulldozer into Stony Fork to widen, deepen and clear it of debris, and in the course of this operation the bulldozer pushed over a dozen big sycamore trees on Caleb's property and tore out a rock wall which his grandpappy had built with slave labor over a hundred years ago.

It is easy enough to see that the damage represented what was at best difficult to set a dollar value on because the value of a sycamore tree growing on the creek bank is difficult to establish and the value of a stone wall built by slave labor is even more difficult to arrive at and maybe impossible. So the thought came to Caleb that since he had a boy in the law school up at Lexington he would just put the matter in his lap and he would know exactly how to handle it. He called his son Jim Henry on the telephone and laid out the problem to him, winding up his discourse by saying "Now Jim Henry me and your Mammy want you to just take off a day from the law school and come down here and make old Judge Tal Strong see daylight."

Jim Henry listened sympathetically to his Daddy's tale of woe concerning the ruination visited upon him by the county road department and then he said "I have only been studying law for less than a year now and we have not yet got to the law covering damage to private property caused by the road department in the course of dredging a creek to provide flood control."

Caleb was understandably disappointed to learn that his son Jim Henry had spent nearly a whole year studying law and hadn't yet got to the point in his studies that would enable him to be helpful to his old Daddy who was in distress because the county had done damage to his property. He was up against county officials in his fight for justice and he was a patient man but he couldn't get them to move no matter how hard he argued with them. He reported to Mattie Belle that he had given them a piece of his mind but he had lost the sycamore trees and the rock wall his grandpappy built to establish the boundary line for as long as the world stands but he had not got anywhere with them.

Jim Henry finished at the law school after three years of study and his graduation coincided with Caleb's next brush with the Law. In fact it was the graduation which brought on the "brush with the Law". Caleb had driven to Lexington to see his son graduate and he became confused in the heavy traffic around the university and wound up driving the wrong way on a one way street. Before he could get off or get turned around he had what is called a "vehicular collision" which means in simple language that he ran into another car.

The worst part of it was that the other car was being driven by a traffic control officer. "I have run into a policeman," Caleb told his son Jim Henry. The damage to the vehicles was slight but the damage to Caleb's self esteem was more than slight; he was devastated. Finding himself in trouble with the Law again he was forced to turn to Jim Henry although he hated to spoil the pleasure of his graduation. Here the boy was all dressed out in his black gown like a judge in a high court room and his Daddy had run into a cop's car. No, that was not the very worst part of it; the worst was that Jim Henry could not help. "I know I'm graduating from the law School today, Dad, but I have not yet passed my bar exams and I couldn't possibly represent you in court."

The upshot of it was that Caleb had to pay a fine for driving the wrong way on a one way street and for being at fault in a collision with a police vehicle which was answering an emergency call and was impeded in the execution of an official duty. His insurance agent was very unfriendly when he was approached about the damages and told Caleb that if this sort of thing occurred again he would be forced to cancel his insurance.

All in all it was a bad time for Caleb but he and Mattie Belle drove back home. "One more dent in the left front fender won't be noticeable on this old jalopy," he said to justify not spending any more money to repair his own car. They were encouraged too with the good news that Jim Henry had landed a good job with a big law firm in Cincinnati. Jim Henry sent a business card with the names Peabody, Hardesty and Esterwhite, Attorneys at Law, emblazoned on it but Caleb could not find Jim Henry's name on the card anywhere. He decided it was enough though that he would receive a good salary and that he would be close enough if he was needed - Cincinnati was only forty or fifty miles away as the crow flies but farther than that on the winding roads that follow the ridges of northern Kentucky. "I am not getting any younger," Caleb said to Mattie Belle, "and I will feel a lot better knowing that Jim Henry will be close by, now that he is a full fledged lawyer."

Mattie Belle did not need to be reminded of the passage of time; she was one year older than Caleb, so she remained silent and only nodded her head but she was glad Jim Henry had a good job in the city. "I would hate for him to have to come back here and open his own law office in competition with old Judge Tal Strong and all the others who have been here since the Flood." When Mattie Bell referred to an event as great as the Deluge she was not talking about the 1937 flood that raised the Ohio River and flooded the city of Louisville. She was talking about the one that inspired Noah to build the Ark.

Caleb said it was certainly a good thing that Jim Henry was close by and with a big law firm that had clout because when Harvey Allbright fell off the barn roof Caleb needed a lawyer. The reason Harvey was on Caleb's barn roof was another natural event that some people refer to as "an act of God." A windstorm had damaged the barn roof and Caleb had hired Harvey to repair it. Why Harvey fell is more difficult to determine and lay at the root of Caleb's need for a lawyer. Harvey claimed the roof was "too damned steep for mortal man to work on and Caleb ought to have knowed better than to send me up there." He claimed to have repaired barn roofs all over the county and had never lost his footing on one before.

Seeing that Harvey was trying to lay the blame on him and make him pay the doctor's and hospital's bills, Caleb claimed that it was because of Harvey's own carelessness and failure to respond to a warning voiced clearly by Caleb himself. "The dern fool laid his hammer down on the barn roof and when it started to slide he lunged at it to ketch it and the next thing you know he was layin' on the ground with his leg broke and all that after I had spoke to him more'n once about layin' his tools around like that."

This was obviously a case that would require adjudication by a third party, which is to say it would go to court and Caleb said to Mattie Belle "It is a good thing we have Jim Henry with that big law firm in Cincinnati or we would lose the farm."

It was with high hopes of being saved from disaster that Caleb turned to his son the lawyer and told him about the predicament.

"Now I just want you to represent me and argue my case in court, Son, and I feel sure we can win it."

Caleb had driven all the way to the city for this visit and he sat in a big chair in Jim Henry's impressive office. Jim Henry gazed sadly into his Daddy's face and said "Gee, Dad, I sure wish I could but I am only licensed to practice law in the state of Ohio and I am not permitted to practice in Kentucky."

"I declare, Mattie Belle," Caleb said as they returned to the ridge farm, "here we have sent this boy off to school to make as fine a lawyer as there is anywhere in the whole country and he has got a good job practisin' law up there in the city and now he ain't worth a plug nickel to us when we need him because they've got a law now against him lawyerin' in Kentucky."

He Made Liars Of Us All

MMiss Florrie asked the Methodist preacher to come and talk to us because ACE was having a bad influence on us and she told Brother Erwin that he might offset this devilish force with an authoritative word from the Source of all good.

It is universally believed by mothers of growing boys that their sons do not get into mischief of their own making nor on their own initiative, but are led into it by some other boy whose evil influence permeates the group as a bad odor spreads through a crowded room. Miss Florrie was the school principal and substitute mother for all the boys and girls in the Colaparchee County Grade School, and she was convinced that much of the mischief that went on there was instigated by ACE who seemed always to be at the head of the pack.

Take for instance the case of the rotten eggs splattered on the transom over the entrance to the school. But that is a story told in detail elsewhere. This is about the preacher's visit for the purpose of counteracting that evil influence.

The Methodist Conference had sent Brother Erwin to Ocmulgee because he was a man of proven integrity and energy and better than average preaching skills, especially when preaching against those evil influences which cause young people to fall into evil ways. His ecclesiastical superior, Bishop Cardigan, was himself a man of both considerable girth and unquestioned probity, and he was deeply concerned about the way the young people were going astray in that modern age when the Great Depression settled upon America, and the bishop was convinced that a just God had sent hard times upon His people to bring them to repentance. Hard times had indeed brought many men

to joblessness, hunger and despair, and the children of those job-
less, hungry and desperate men looked about themselves to see
what they could do to divert and entertain themselves, without
any thought of how their action might lift America out of the
Depression.

But the evil ways which beckoned to us at Colaparchee Grade
School were mostly hearsay. We had heard them from ACE who
claimed to have done all the forbidden things and to have
escaped unscathed, except for a few paddlings by Miss Florrie
who wielded the Orangewood Board of Education. Even this did
not faze ACE; he carried the paddlings the way a hero bears the
wounds and scars of war. A righteous war at that.

But Miss Florrie engaged the Methodist preacher to talk to us
and he came one cold, wet February morning, parking his little
English Ford as close to the building as he could get on account
of the inclement weather. Then he stood on the porch as we lined
up ,n the cold drizzle to march inside. At the signal from Miss
Florrie we ascended the steps, marched into the auditorium and
stood at attention . We saluted the Flag and pledged allegiance;
we repeated the Lord's Prayer and sat down.

Miss Florrie then sent the smaller children to their classes and
kept grades five, six and seven for some special attention. She
introduced Brother Erwin and turned him loose on us. He told
us about Satan's devices for luring us into the flaming pit.
Smoking was one of them, but just an introductory one. After
smoking came using bad language and drinking whiskey. But
dancing was the real danger zone because of what it could lead
to, especially if we had been drinking and had our moral sensi-
bilities dulled by alcohol.

What it could lead to was an unwanted pregnancy for a girl
and a horrible disease for a boy, plus a life time guilt trip for having forfeited the chance to enter marriage as an unblemished virgin. This was the part that interested us most, since we were at
that age when both boys and girls have an insatiable curiosity
about sex, and are driven to inquire, explore and experiment in
the hope that their childish dabblings will enable them to find
out why their elders so jealously guard the secrets.

But Brother Erwin did not omit warnings against lying, cheat-
ing on tests, stealing watermelons, and committing acts of violence and destruction of property. We assumed that Miss Florrie

had told him about the egg battle on the front steps of the school-
house, involving ACE, Junior and me. We were all duly
impressed by these threats to our happiness on this earth and to
future bliss in the world to come, but Brother Erwin did not let
us off with being duly impressed. He made us take THE
PLEDGE.

Taking the pledge meant that we stood with bowed heads and
closed eyes and were told to raise our hands as pledge of our
agreement not to do any of the bad things we had been told
about, so we swore not to smoke, drink, cuss, dance or engage in
bodily contact with the opposite sex. This last pledge was binding upon us up to the marriage altar. After that we were free to
do what comes naturally with God's approval, so long as we did
it with the person we had gone to the marriage altar with.

I told you we took the pledge with eyes closed but I cheated. I
opened my right eye just a crack of the eyelid to see whose hands
had gone up on that side; then I did the same with the left and I
saw that everybody was taking the Pledge. Even ACE. In fact,
ACE not only had his hand up; he was waving it about over his
head with unbounded enthusiasm to let Brother Erwin know
that he, ACE, was the most devout of the devotees of righteousness, purity and abstinence from evil doing.

After we had all taken the Pledge Brother Erwin prayed, giving the Lord a glowing report of his success and then leaving the
hard job of keeping us on the straight and narrow up to God
Whose Eye is on the sparrow and is never closed. Then we went
to our classroom and in the confusion ACE disappeared.

Miss Florrie did not notice at first because she had lingered to
talk with the preacher and congratulate him on a job well done
and she was anxious to get back to the classroom but Brother
Erwin was loath to leave the place of moral victory over Satan, so
Miss Florrie was gone from the classroom longer than she
deemed it wise. ACE was slipping into his seat on the row next
to the blackboard when she came in and started assigning work
in the arithmetic workbook. She gave ACE a hard look but before
she could reprimand him for being out of his seat Brother Erwin
came to the door and motioned to her. Then he told her that all
four tires on his car were as flat as a flitter and did anyone have a
pump and maybe a boy to do the pumping.

"Yes" Miss Florrie said. "I keep a pump in the luggage compartment to my car and ACE will do the pumping. It will be good exercise for him and may help him to keep his pledge in the future." ACE's performance on the hand pump brought the sweat out on his face even though it was a cold, raw February day. And when all four tires were standing up again Brother Erwin made him take the Pledge again, repeating the preacher's words after him like the groom in the wedding ceremony.

Not many of us who took the Pledge were able to persevere in righteousness because the wiles of the devil are beyond the strength of a growing boy to resist. But it must have brought great joy in heaven for as long as it lasted. And surely the devil felt some satisfaction in seeing that it didn't last long with ACE.

One of the preacher's tires went down again before he got home because ACE had loosened the valve core while Brother Ervin was starting up the engine. ACE also took the connector cap off Miss Florrie's pump and hid it under the spare tire but she didn't miss it until the day she needed it.

The Night The Moon
Turned To Blood

B rother Stranglewood made his startling announcement on the third night of the brush arbor meeting. "The world is coming to an end tonight, Brothers and Sisters," Brother Stranglewood declared, holding his open, black imitation leather bound Bible in his left hand so that the two sections held apart by his thumb fell limply over his upraised hand.

With his right hand he pointed to the brothers and sisters for whom this apocalyptic event held the greatest threat. "It tells us right here in God's Holy Word that when the moon is turned to blood the world will come to an end."

Brother Stranglewood had not been able to find the Scripture passage that actually said the moon would turn to blood but he had found the one that said the moon would fail to give its light. That was in the Gospel of Matthew, chapter 24 and verse 29, and that was good enough because the moon was growing smaller by the minute and it was obvious to him and to any observer with good eyes that at this rate it would soon disappear altogether.

Anyway, he reasoned, blood is mentioned throughout the Bible, and how could a man do better than to call upon that magical power by just coming right out and saying that the moon was being turned to blood?

Striding back and forth across the makeshift platform Brother Stranglewood spoke as the prophet of doom. "Look up into the heavens. Yes, lift up your eyes and behold God's sign in the sky. And hear His terrible word from the Holy Bible."

High over the leafy canopy that stood as the only barrier between the hundreds of worshipers and the judgment of God rode a blood red and steadily diminishing moon.

"Repent my brothers and sisters!" Brother Stranglewood cried. "Oh Sinners! Repent! Before you fall into the hands of an angry God! Repent now and make your profession of faith for the Day of judgment is at hand!"

Adoniram Judson Stranglewood was an imposing figure of a man. Six feet two inches tall. A hundred and ninety pounds. Coal black hair flowing like a mane onto his neck. Blazing black eyes above a blade like nose. Mouth wide and full of pearly white teeth. Except for one gold tooth that flashed and glinted in the lantern light of the arbor. Ad Stranglewood wore a suit of black broadcloth as befitted an evangelist of wide reputation. A starched white shirt and a narrow black tie.

But that was when he started out. That was when he entered the pulpit. Bible in hand. As he worked himself into his sermon he worked himself out of his clerical garb. First the coat, which he laid aside carefully. Then the tie which he pulled down, leaving it knotted about his neck but hanging loosely on his heaving chest. So that by the time he reached the alarming aspect of his pronouncement, Brother Stranglewood was in his shirt sleeves and bathed in sweat. Not the polite form of perspiration. Real he man sweat. Sweat as befits a preacher of the Word of God.

"Repent! For the Day of His Wrath, yea, the Night of His judgment, is at hand!"

When he had made this pronouncement the preacher looked with greater fierceness at the men and women and children huddled in fear under the brush arbor. Suddenly he lifted his eyes to watch the approach of two young men marching with deliberate tread down the aisle to face Brother Stranglewood. They were Larry Eversole and Tracy Johnson, both of them very serious of mein and both feeling the great importance of their mission, for they had been outside to peer into the sky at the moon without the leafy branches of the arbor to obstruct their vision. Now they were returning to report to Brother Stranglewood that the moon was growing smaller and bloodier by the minute. Brother Stranglewood bent his dark head to receive their report, for he was a head taller than the two young sun burned farmers turned moon watchers.

Brother Stranglewood raised his face and opened his mouth to report to the gathered faithful the unhappy news that the situation was becoming more perilous but Sister Sarah Updyke chose that moment to give vent to her own religious fervor. With a piercing scream she rose from the split rail bench where she was sitting with her young husband and their four small children. She sent the flimsy seat tumbling over by the violence of her motion as she propelled herself toward Brother Stranglewood.

Sarah's husband and her four children managed to get the bench upright again and resume their seats as she rushed forward on a collision course with the young men who stood between her and Brother Stranglewood. They quickly moved aside and Sister Sarah threw herself onto the ground at Brother Stranglewood's feet and cried out in a high keening voice "No! Blessed Lord Jesus! Not yet! Save me and my children before the fire of judgment falls on our heads!"

It was probably a matter of simple oversight and not a deliberate omission that she had left her young husband Nathan Updyke out of her plea for mercy and salvation. No matter though. For Nathan was too busy containing the aroused emotions of the four children to notice.

Sarah Updyke was a woman of uncommon natural beauty and religious fervor. At twenty six she had attained the full blossoming of womanhood, the opening of which had begun nine years earlier when she responded to Nate Updyke's passionate declarations of love with an ardor that matched his own, with the result that their matched passion and ardor had produced one little Updyke the first year of their marriage and another every second year thereafter. Sarah Updyke also experienced a great religious upheaval every other summer at the revival meetings, called protracted meetings because they were extended until the harvest season came on and forced the farm folk to give up the entertainment and go back to work in the fields.

The reason Sister Sarah got a violent case of religion every other summer was that she was pregnant every second year. Usually about two or three months pregnant when the big meeting took place. But on this occasion when the moon was turned to blood she was far enough gone to be showing prominently, and this would have occasioned concern on the part of wise old grannies, had it not been for the announcement that the world was coming to an end and so why worry about a few violent exertions bringing on a premature birth?

Retrospectively it was the pregnancy that brought on the outpouring of religious fervor. Sarah's first child, Caleb, was conceived before the marriage vows were spoken publicly and it was the recurrent remembrance of this that brought on Sarah's biennial prostrations. But never before had she had so compelling a reason to prostrate herself before the Lord as the bloody moon had given in that year of the mid-thirties. Nor had she ever had such a figure of a Man of God to represent the Divine Presence as Adoniram Judson Stranglewood, Evangelist of Note and Reputation, did on the night the moon was turned to blood.

Sarah Updyke's demonstration of religious zeal, while it was singularly impressive in itself, was of far reaching significance because hers was not the only such action but rather the herald, the torch bearer which touched off with its own spark, the mass movement of repentant sinners streaming to the altar of God. For soon after her first outcries, they began moving, at first one here and one there, then twos and threes and then bunches until almost everybody under the brush arbor had come to the fount of Divine Mercy, or as near as they could get, which was becoming more difficult as they crowded around the preacher. Almost, but not all of them; there was one notorious holdout. Jonathan Birdsong was an onlooker. An observer and a commentator on the religious phenomenon rather than a participant. Untouched by it, Jonathan reported on it; it was Jonathan who defined Sarah Updyke's role in it.

"They all set there like so many bumps on a log till that little fireball jumped up and threw her petticoats to the winds and then they all caught fire and before anybody knowed what was happening all hell had busted loose and there ain't no preacher on Earth and maybe not even a God in Heaven could stop'em from bein' a part of what was happenin' to her.

"Yeah, I reckon one little spark from the altars of paganism would have set off the damnedest orgy you ever seen."

Whatever truth or fallacy or mere exaggeration may attach to Jonathan Birdsong's analysis of revival meetings under a brush arbor, it soon became evident to Brother Stranglewood that the Lord had moved His people beyond human control and he called upon them to be still while he sought the Lord's direction in prayer and when he had prayed fervently and long he announced that the Lord had spoken and given him a sign for His people.

"The world is going to end tonight," he reaffirmed.

"And before the sun rises tomorrow all the prophecies in the Book of Revelations will be fulfilled. But many of you have come here tonight leaving loved ones and family members at home to face the Wrath of God alone. The thing for all of you to do now is return to your homes and be re-united with your families and. loved ones. If any one of you has sinned against any one be reconciled through confession and forgiveness so that you may face your Maker with a clean heart. Go now, while there is still time for you to reach your homes and face the Judgment with your arms about your own beloved family members."

Some of them wanted to make their confession on the spot, fearing that Judgment might fall before they reached the ones they had offended. One man confessed to having moved a boundary line between himself and his neighbor and he promised to replace the markers if God would spare him long enough. "I'm goin' home right now and set that matter right," he promised the preacher.

Another, a merchant, admitted he had overcharged and short changed a customer who hadn't the wit to catch it. "I'll never do it again," he declared but he did not say he would give the money back to the fellow he had cheated.

And one penitent husband cried out that he had been unfaithful to his wife. She overheard him and replied that she had cheated on him too. Brother Stranglewood stood there staring at the two of them, not knowing what to say or do, so he urged them all again to be on their way home.

They made a hasty exodus from the brush arbor. Men and women gathering their broods of children and loading them into wagons and buggies. Some young blades had come on horseback and they mounted now in great haste, causing the horses to rear and plunge amidst the wagons. This resulted in great confusion and some eloquent outbursts of profanity.

One or two fancy carriages were to be found among the humbler conveyances, and the drivers of these attempted to steer clear of the mass of people, mules, horses and wheeled vehicles but they were not entirely successful. One fine carriage was jammed up against the hub of a farm wagon and the owner was quite upset over the damage done to the carriage.

Some even of the humbler pilgrims were afoot and these were

able to quickly get ahead of their mule and horse drawn fellows but they were soon overtaken and left in the dust by them once they got clear of the traffic jam at the brush arbor.

Among those making a hasty departure was Oliver Hainsworth father of five, some of whom were difficult to find in the darkness and confusion. While he was putting the mules into their traces he was calling out to his wife Amy. "You round up them damn' younguns and let's git outta here. We left my pore old Mammy at home and she's got the lumbago so bad she can't hardly walk, let alone run. We got to git home in a hurry."

When the Hainsworths were all present and accounted for they set off at a trot but when they had gone about two miles a trace chain on the mule on the right came loose from the single tree and this brought the whole equipage to a halt right in front of Jeb Arnold's Country Crossroads Store, and as Lady Luck, or a Divine Providence would have it, Jeb had kept the store open late because he expected some trade from the farmers returning from the brush arbor meeting.

"For God's sake Jeb!" Oliver Hainsworth cried out. "Bring me a lantern here and help me git this trace chain fixed. The world's comin' to a end tonight and I have got to git home to die with my pore old Mammy who's there all alone."

"What in hell are you talkin' about Oliver?" Jeb thought Oliver might have gone crazy. "Who told you the world's coming to an end tonight?"

"The preacher. He read it right outta the Bible and there's the sign of it right up there in the sky; don't you see that bloody moon up there?"

Oliver pointed toward the sky but by this time the moon had disappeared altogether and he stood aghast at the prospect of immediate destruction.

"Oh Bull Shit Oliver!" Jeb exclaimed. "The world ain't coming to no end. Look here." And Jeb grabbed up a copy of the Memphis Appeal. "There's a front page story here about the eclipse of the moon. Ain't nothin' for you to be in such a swivet about. Just calm down and wait until tomorrow night and you'll see the same old moon a sailin' through the sky like ain't nothin' ever happened to it."

Jeb hooked a link of the trace chain into the clevis on the single tree and turned to go back into the store.

"Trouble with you Oliver is you take what ever' Tom Fool preacher says serious when you oughtta be readin' the newspaper."

Brother Stranglewood had a bad day in the aftermath of the night the moon was turned to blood.

Those believers who had confessed their sins in the expectation of the end of the World found themselves facing the people they had sinned against. In the bright light of day the sinned against were not eager to forgive

Jake Hargis was not happy about having confessed his infidelity to his wife Ophelia and Ophelia was not happy about having admitted that she was guilty of the same sin. The worse part of it was that Ophelia now hated the woman Jake had named, whereas she had formerly considered her a good friend. But the worst part was that she now suspected that her one time friend was not the only one and so she was suspicious of every woman who had been close to them. And Jake vowed that he would kill the man Ophelia had named, and any others who turned up on the list under questioning.

Needless to say, Ophelia Hargis would never trust Jake out of her sight again. And Jake Hargis would never trust Ophelia again. Since they no longer trusted one another out of sight, nor enjoyed one another's company, they were, in Jake's words "damned if they did and damned if they didn't."

Both Jake and Ophelia blamed Brother Stranglewood for their predicament and accused him of being a false prophet because his prediction of the end of the world had not come to pass and they were left to pick up the scraps of their sinful lives.

Tom Thistlewaite had publicly confessed that he had moved a boundary line and he was caught red handed so to speak working by the light of a lantern setting the fence back where it was supposed to be. Homer Jackson, the neighbor who had lost the use of a strip of ground ten feet wide and four hundred feet long and hadn't noticed it for seven years, saw the light moving about on the back side of his farm at midnight and he grabbed his shotgun and went to investigate. When he found his neighbor digging post holes he was surprised to say the least and he said "My God, Tom, tell me what in hell you think you're doing."

When Tom told him he was trying to avert final judgment and the wrath of an angry God, Homer said " I had better help you if you aim to get the job done before sunup." At sunup both of them returned to Homer's house where Homer called to his wife and said "Tom here says the world's comin' to a end any minute now. You hurry up and put breakfast on the table. I don't wanta meet my Maker on a empty stomach after diggin' post holes all night."

After a hearty breakfast of ham and grits and fried eggs Tom and Homer were having their second cup of coffee and the world was still standing, so Homer said "Jest outta curiosity Tom, how come you wanted that strip of no account ground? It won't grow nothin' but weeds nohow."

Then Tom said "Well you know that big ol' hickor' nut tree that stands just over the line on your side? I allus was crazy about hickor' nuts and that's how come I moved the line."

"My God Tom!" Homer sipped his coffee and it burned his tongue. "If I hadda knowed I wouldha give you the hickor' nuts. I ain't got my own teeth no more and I can't crack 'em."

The events which took place on the boundary line between Tom Thistlewaite and Homer Jackson were reported by a third neighbor, Nellie Bifer, who embellished the story by saying that she had heard that both men were "bad put out at the preacher for making them lose a night's sleep and they vowed that they would never give another dime to him or any other preacher if they lived to be as old as Methusalah and witnessed the real end of the whole creation."

This was relayed to Brother Stranglewood about mid-morning just as he picked up his Bible to search for the reason he had miscalculated the time of the End of the World.

Honest John Dawkins, the merchant who had cheated his feeble minded customer, returned to his store on the morning after the moon was turned to blood. He unlocked the door, went inside and set out his merchandise; then he waited, but nobody showed up to purchase his wares. Normally, business was brisk in the early morning hours because farm folks always thought of something they needed from the store and they expected Honest John to be open and waiting at daybreak. But by nine o'clock he had seen one customer, an old black man called Uncle Mose. This grizzled patriarch of the colored community had not been at the brush arbor meeting because the coloreds were not allowed to attend religious services with the whites.

Uncle Mose came in his ignorance of the impending doom of the night before; he bought a plug of chewing tobacco and commented on the emptiness of Honest John 's General Store. "Where ever' body at Mister John?" he asked and Honest John busied himself with straightening up a stack of canned goods but he made no reply. Uncle Mose went out chewing the tobacco with a few scraggly front teeth because he had lost all of his jaw teeth.

At noon the storekeeper went home to lunch but he had no appetite, and afterwards he lay down and tried to take a short nap as was his custom, but with no success. After forty minutes of restless turning he got up and went in search of Brother Stranglewood who was staying at the widow Turner's while the meeting was going on.

Honest John Dawkins found Brother Stranglewood sitting on the porch, brooding on last night's debacle and searching the pages of his Bible for a text that he might use that evening to explain why the world had not come to an end.

The merchant walked up to the evangelist and without an exchange of civilities he said "God dammit Preacher you have ruint my business. Now instidda lookin' fer a text for tonight you had better git outta this county before you are rode outta here on a pole."

The foregoing incidents were by no means all of the unhappy occurrences in the life of Brother Stranglewood on the day after the lunar eclipse, but they are sufficient to set the stage for what took place when Hank Mayberry came over and said he had decided to marry Sadie Birdsong and he had fifty cents in his pocket which he proposed to give to Brother Stranglewood in payment for tying the knot in true ministerial fashion.

Hank Mayberry was not much brighter than it is required for a man to be able to walk and chew gum at the same time hut there are some things that seem to come naturally to men and women without the need for formal instruction or a high IQ, and when Hank came to make his request of Brother Stranglewood he confessed to him that he and Sadie had been living together for three years without having gone to the trouble and extra expense of a wedding ceremony. This confession was not necessary because they had already produced two offspring in their own image as proof that they knew what to do without being told. Sadie's bulging belly indicated that they had not forgotten what they already knew.

"But me an' Sadie we got to thinkin' after your sermon last night that we might be livin' in sin and if the Judgment Day did ketch us doin' it we might jest go straight to hell for it without no chance to do nothin' about it."

A small boy child was tagging along, hanging to Sadie's skirt and peering out from behind at the preacher man; she held a nursing baby of indeterminate age at her breast, The baby's feet kicked her swollen stomach when it applied itself to the business of getting nourishment. Sadie stood silent while her groom to be talked with Brother Stranglewood.

It had not occurred to Hank and Sadie that they would need a license to make the ceremony legal and binding, and when Brother Stranglewood brought this to their attention Hank said "I'll run into town and try to ketch 'em before they close the Court House. Maybe I can git back here in time for you to marry us up before you go to the brush arbor meetin' tonight Preacher."

But Brother Stranglewood was not feeling in the festive mood appropriate for tying the marital knot. He sat there on the widow's porch half listening to Hank and with his hands thumbing through the Good Book in search of a text that he might use at the brush arbor that evening. Hank and Sadie and the little ones were waiting patiently for him to say he would marry them as soon as Hank could get back with the license.

"I tell you what, Hank," Brother Stranglewood said, still flipping pages in his Bible. "You and Sadie have been living this way for about three or four years now and the Lord has just spoke to me and told me that since the Judgment Day has been put off indefinitely, it won't matter now if you wait another day or two."

He stopped flipping pages and looked straight at Hank. But the two of you're living in sin and I am gonna speak for the Lord in this and say you ought to sleep one of you on one side of the bed and the other on the other side as far apart as you can manage to get until you get that marriage license and get married up proper and legal the way the Good Book says."

The Glue Pot

Herman Gooseberry became Superintendent of the Scarrsville independent School District on his fifty fourth birthday. He said it was God's birthday present to him, and he saw the job as an opportunity and a: responsibility to honor and glorify God the Creator of Heaven and Earth, Scarrsville Kentucky being a very special focal point of God's concern for the Earth.

Herman had entertained the idea in his youthful days that God had called him to be a preacher but when he tried it nobody listened. The reason for this is that Herman was a very boring speaker and as a consequence of the lack of evangelical fire on his tongue, no church was inclined to hire' him to do the preaching. It is a fortunate union of events when both God and His church call a man to preach, but these two events did not come together in the life of Herman Gooseberry and he decided to become a school teacher instead of a preacher because it was necessary to make a living at something and it seemed to Herman the only open avenue to a steady income without engaging in hard manual work, a prospect which did not appeal to him at all.

When he had been teaching in third grade classroom for twelve years Herman became keenly aware that people in the administrative area of education are better paid than classroom teachers. Besides, he observed that they do not have to put up with noisy students all day and then spend their evenings grading papers at home. He had saved up some money which he then spent by going back to the University to earn a Master's degree and he began pulling strings and pushing buttons which eventually brought him to the job of superintendent, a circumstance which was helped along by the Death angel who touched

Harvey Klondike, the old superintendent in the middle of one cold February night, leaving the Scarrsville Schools without a leader. Herman, meanwhile, had mentioned his conviction that God had him in mind for the job; he had mentioned this to members of the school board, so when Harvey was found dead in his bed instead of seated at his desk the morning after this fateful night, Herman was chosen by a majority of the school board members to fill his empty shoes and he rejoiced, giving praise to God and promising to honor and glorify Him in any way he could.

The opportunity to do this presented itself when the science book was shown to Herman by an irate parent who declared that the text book being used by the sixth grade students was fostering godless atheism and ought to be barred from the classroom.

Superintendent Gooseberry had not looked at the sixth grade science textbook but when Johnny Furbeloe's parent invited him to open the book to pages 172 and 173 he found himself staring right into the face of the Big Bang Theory of the Creation of the Universe, of which the planet Earth is a small but significant part, being the locus of Scarrsville Kentucky where Superintendent Gooseberry now occupied the large chair behind the large desk once occupied by Harvey Klondike, now deceased.

The big Bang Theory is that a relatively small but very compact ball of matter reached such a stage of density and degree of heated activity that it just exploded with a Big Bang, scattering everywhere and becoming suns and moons and stars and planets, one of which is known as Earth and is inhabited by Man and other forms of life. But nowhere in the Big Bang Theory is there any intimation that God had a hand in it while it is clearly stated in the first two chapters of Genesis which is the first of '66 books comprising the Bible, that God did. it all just by speaking the Word. Except for the very crown of creation, Man, in whose creation God actually got His hands muddy because he took some of the Earth and formed a Man, out of whom He made a Woman. Superintendent Gooseberry believed that this was not only the first but the last word in Creation.

Upon examining the science text book it was evident to the Superintendent that the parent of Johnny Furbeloe was right. The Big Bang Theory was a contradiction of Bible Truth, and to teach the Big Bang Theory as the explanation for the creation of the whole universe was to spit into the Face of God. So Superintendent Gooseberry began to look for a way to correct the situation.

The first solution which he considered was to get rid of offending science books which taught the Big Bang Theory and replace them with Bibles, the King James Version preferred, with the true account of God's creation of the world and man too.

This easy solution received short shrift with the canny superintendent for he saw that it would involve him in a law suit. The Supreme Court had already ruled against Bible reading in the schools and Superintendent Gooseberry knew that the Supreme Court is a more formidable adversary than a Furbeloe. Besides, there was the matter of fiscal responsibility to be considered and the superintendent was a firm believer in fiscal responsibility. On several occasions he had made the statement "Waste not, want not" and although he had not been required to explain what that meant, it was plainly evident that the text books had been bought and paid for, and besides, they contained a lot of good stuff which would be thrown away with the Big Bang Theory on pages 172 and 173.

For instance, there was the chapter on Locomotion, which didn't seem to be in conflict with Bible Truth. Why throw away Locomotion with the Big Bang Theory and subject himself to charges of wastefulness by the good people of Scarrsville and by the School Board members who were privileged to look over the budget?

He next considered tearing out, or cutting out neatly with a sharp razor blade,, the two offending pages. Then he realized that this would create a new problem. Two new problems, to be exact. Page 172 was the back side of page 171 which was the last page of the chapter dealing with locomotion. He had noticed that while flipping the pages to find the story of the Big Bang. Also, page 173 was the front side of page 174 which dealt with rainfall, and while the chapter on rainfall did not expressly attribute rainfall to an act of God in response to prayer, it didn't deny it either, but merely described the action of clouds and air and gave the technical aspects of it without implying that God does not cause the rain to fall on the just and the unjust alike. As a matter of fact, for a just God to behave in that manner about rain would have been a puzzler to say the least, to the mind of Superintendent Gooseberry, if he had put his mind to the matter.

So if pages 172-173 were cut out, then pages 171 and 174 would be sacrificed and the two chapters on Locomotion and Rain fall would be mangled, one at the end and the other at the beginning, leaving the students wondering about the end of the story on Locomotion and the beginning of Rainfall.

It was in a near fit of exasperation that Superintendent Gooseberry slammed the science textbook down on his large desk and in doing so he upset a small jar of glue which he had been using to attach some pictures of the school's football team to the pages of a scrapbook. The jar of glue fell over onto the carpet and made quite a mess which the Superintendent tried to clean up with his handkerchief but succeeded only in making a bigger mess and finally had to call the janitor who preferred to be called the custodian, to clean it up. But the Lord speaks to His servants in mysterious ways through the most unlikely events, and Superintendent Gooseberry received a revelation in the upsetting of the jar of glue.

"This is it!" he exclaimed, and he called for a pot of glue and for helpers from both the administrative and the teaching staff. "Spread the glue on pages 172-173," he directed them. "Press the pages together firmly until they are thoroughly stuck. That will fix the Big Bang Theory without bringing the Supreme Court down on us for teaching Biblical Creation. We'll just move on from Locomotion to Rainfall and nobody will know the difference."

While the teachers and administrative staff stared at him in amazement, the superintendent added "We will just glue the pages together and that will be the end of it."

It was not the end of it; it was only the beginning. The press got hold of the story and it appeared in the Scarsville Clarion under the headline! School Superintendent Drops the Big Bang in the Glue Pot. When the story reached the citizens of Scarrsville, reaction was mixed. Religious zealots enthusiastically endorsed the superintendent's action; one of these zealots, Jake Johnson, a member of the School Board, said "I agree fully with Superintendent Gooseberry's action. if we can't teach that God created the world the way the Bible says He did, we won't teach the Big Bang Theory."

Professor Nathan Stokeley, head of the Science Department at the Scarrsville Junior College, said "Gooseberry's action is ridiculous. You can't suppress scientific endeavor by dipping it in a glue pot." The local clergy were divided on the issue. The Reverend David Horner, minister of the Presbyterian church, said "There is no conflict between science and the Biblical myth of creation." But Brother Jimmy Waiters, the Baptist preacher, reacted vehemently to the use of the term "myth" in reference to the Genesis account of creation.

Brother Jimmy preached a sermon from his pulpit on the Sunday morning following the news story. "Hell will be full of unbelievers who call the Bible a book of myths!" he declared.

Students in the sixth grade were the ones who came up with the solution to the matter. They steamed open pages 172-173 so they could read the forbidden story of the Big Rang, but when they had read it they were just as mystified as they were before they read it. Little Jimmy Abernathy asked his teacher "Where did God get the little ball of stuff that blew up?"

Most of the students were a bit fuzzy from sniffing the glue though and they went outside on the school playground and started a baseball game. Tim O'Leary hit a heroic home run in the ninth inning and this feat was hailed as a Big Bang.

To Paint A Mailbox

Oscar was deep in thought. His hand, scribbling almost illegibly, flew across the page of the yellow pad in front of his intense, fiercely burning eyes. Thoughts raced through his head even faster than the moving hand could write. This was it! He had puzzled long and pondered deeply the writings of Goethe, Germany's epic poet. What had he really been saying in his FAUST? And now he had it; he must get it down in the exact words, concise, yet fully explicit, for the Book Club.

This time he would tell them what nobody else had ever told them, or even written, about Goethe's Faust. Then Ethel touched him lightly on the shoulder. He looked up, not actually seeing her, just reacting to her touch. She was standing close beside him. She said "Uncle Roy says he is willing to come and paint the mail box if we want him to."

He saw her, heard her, drew a deep breath as unnoticeably as it is possible to draw a deep breath when one is exasperated. "That's great!" he said (An oxymoron.) "Your Uncle .Roy is a painter." (An obvious statement.)

"I told Uncle Roy we had to put our new 911 address on the mailbox and he said he would come over and paint it for us if we want him to do it." She paused. It was becoming evident to Oscar that she had ASKED Uncle Roy to paint the mailbox or else she had hinted at it so broadly he felt constrained to offer to do it.

After the pause, "It doesn't look like you are ever going to get around to doing it." She looked at the culpable yellow pad.

It was now harder for him to hide his exasperation because he was losing Faust, Mephistopheles, Gretchen and the whole cast of characters. "Why don't you just tell your Uncle Roy that we'll be glad for him to paint the mail box?"

"He wouldn't charge anything and it has to be done anyway because they have changed our address for 911. It will have to be done anyway and he's offered to do it for us."

Now Goethe himself was gone with the entire cast of his epic poem, or play, or whatever the hell it was by now. "Let Uncle Roy paint the mail box then." A note of anger had crept into his voice while he stared at the yellow pad on the writing table in front of him.

"Well, he'll be over here in about an hour but you'll have to clean it up first. I wouldn't want Uncle Roy to have to work on it dirty the way it is."

"Maybe Uncle Roy would like to prepare the mailbox for painting the way he wants it. He's the painter, you know." He was tapping the yellow pad ominously with the ball point pen.

She recoiled at this suggestion. "If we're going to ask my Uncle Roy to come over here and paint our mail box the least you could do is go out there and clean it up for him before he gets here."

"WE haven't asked your Uncle Roy to do anything. I'll paint the damned mail box myself when I get around to it." He was working up a sweat and tapping the yellow pad more rapidly. Goethe and his people were gone to hell with the devil to turn over their souls to him. She was becoming angry to cover her hurt. "That's what you always say and then you never get around to doing it. The least you could do if Uncle Roy is nice enough to come and paint it is..."

"All right dammit! I'll go right now and wash the bird shit off the mail box so your Uncle Roy won't get his fingers in it while he's painting."

She recoiled from this angry outburst. "Oh no. I don't want you to touch it. Don't leave your desk and your precious writing project. I'll do it myself. You just go back to writing. Or whatever you were doing."

"Go back to my writing, you say!? It's all blown to hell out of my head now!" He slammed the pen down on the yellow pad, stormed out of the house, bucket in hand, had to come back and find a towel, run water into the bucket from the end of the hose attached to the water outlet on the side of the house. He washed the bird lime off the mail box. When he'd finished he breathed deeply, came back to his work room and began the search for Faust and Mephistopheles. After about twenty minutes he found them in Gretchen's jail cell but he couldn't remember what was the special insight he had gained into what Goethe's Faust was saying about the illusory nature of love.

Uncle Roy arrived forty eight minutes later, paint brush and can in hand. He was in a jovial mood and seemed pleased to see Oscar who had come out to meet him near the mail box. Ethel had remained inside the house, doing whatever women do when they have won a Pyrrhic victory.

"Yep," Uncle Roy said, stirring the paint with a small twig he had picked up from the ground near the mailbox. "It needs painting real bad. It's been a while since I painted it the last time."

Oscar couldn't remember how long a while it had been since the last time but he was confident he would remember the date of this painting. It was June the second, 1996. A hot day with a thunderhead gathering in the Southwestern sky.

And The Goat Cried

"Your Mama's right, Son," Papa said, sniffing the wind. "Something's got to be done about that damn goat. When the wind blows toward the house you can smell him a mile away."

"I wish he was a mile away instead of standing in the front yard." Mama waved her apron in front of her nose to waft away Billy's odor. "I never wanted you to bring a goat here anyway. Now all he does is stand there bleating all day long and stinking up the place."

"Well, a boy ought to have a goat once in his life time." Papa was always defensive about any bad decision he had ever made. "This one just didn't turn out to he much good at pulling a goat cart. But we got to do something about that God-awful smell. Can't put up with it much longer with hot weather coming on. The place'll smell so bad we can't sit on the front porch."

I studied Papa's face but I couldn't find in it the answer to my question. "What are we gonna do, Papa? Ain't no use givin' Billy a bath. When it rains on him he just smells worse'n ever." I was awed by Billy's imposing presence and his belligerent stance. Ever since the day he had wrecked the goat cart I had known I would never tame this goat but I was not willing to give up either.

The "wreck" was an embarrassment to Papa too because when Papa built a goat cart he meant to take a ride in it. And he didn't mean for the goat to determine either the direction of the ride or the duration of it. But Billy had outsmarted Papa.

The excursion was going pretty well until we reached the end of the driveway and started to turn into the county road. That was when Irvin Haygood's milk truck came rumbling past and frightened Billy. "Scared the daylights outta him," Papa had told Mama when she demanded an account of our escapade. "All them empty milk cans a rattlin' and a bangin' together like judgment day and Irvin drivin' forty miles an hour on that washboard road."

To Billy, Irvin Haygood's milk truck was the embodiment of all the bad things that are to be avoided by goats. And the security of the barn he had so recently left suddenly became very attractive to him. He whirled and dashed madly toward the barn and it was all Papa could do to keep the cart from overturning.

"Hang on, Boys!" Papa yelled and Junior and I clung to the goat cart while Papa tugged at the lines to keep Billy from dashing the cart against a fence post. We swung into the barn lot at full speed and then Billy slowed down a little but he didn't come to a halt; instead he crouched, still running, and went for the opening under the barn which was set on rock pillars about two feet high. This was high enough for Billy to go under but not high enough for the goat cart, with Papa and Junior and me to follow him. The cart struck the barn a jolting blow. Papa and Junior and I were all thrown from the cart. The harness was stripped off Billy who retreated into the shadows under the barn. The left front wheel of the goat cart hung crazily to its axle, spinning slowly out of kilter.

"Damn' Billy Goat!" Papa exclaimed, looking all around to see if anybody was hurt. "You boys go to the house and get your Mama to check you over good and make sure you ain't got no broken bones. When I git done with that goat there might be some out here."

Not Billy's bones. Papa couldn't get Billy to come out from under the barn until the next day. By that time Papa had cooled down some but when he did catch Billy he tied him to a stake in the front yard to graze. "And to stink up the whole neighborhood," Mama said, more unhappy than ever about Billy because of the wreck of the goat cart with all of us in it.

That was when Papa had to face up to Mama's ultimatum. "You do something to stop that goat from stinking or you get rid of the goat."

"But what can you do to stop him from stinkin' Papa?" I asked. "Ain't it just his natural smell?"

"Well Son," Papa said, "it's the nature of a goat to smell bad.

That's sure the God's truth. But there is something a man can do about it. I just hate to do it."

"What's that, Papa? How come you hate to do it?" I never had noticed that Papa hated to do anything if he saw it had to be done.

"Well, I just hate to cut a goat. Now you take a hull calf and cut him and he bawls a while and mopes around for a day or two but if you can keep the blow flies off him he's all right. Even a pig. You just turn him upside down in a oil drum and he squeals his head off for two minutes and that's the end of it. But a goat is a different proposition."

"Proposition or what not," Mama said, getting provoked with Papa's shilly shallying around about the goat. "I'm tired of smelling that goat. I know a goat's got feelings too but if you are not going to do something about the smell, you can just get rid of him. If you can't sell him, give him away. There ought to be somebody crazy enough to take him and turn him loose in the creek swamp."

"I never had to give anything away to git rid of it in my life," Papa said. "And I don't aim to start now by givin' away a perfectly good goat." Papa paused and studied Billy who was chewing his cud and exuding a strong odor. "If it's come to that I'm just goin' to have to operate on him."

"What kind of operation are you gonna do on him, Papa?" My eyes were big with wonder now. "Are you gonna put Billy to sleep and operate on him the way the doctor did me when he took out my 'pendix?"

"I wish I was goin' to put him to sleep." Papa's voice sounded remorseful already. "It would be a heap easier on everybody. Especially ol' Billy. But I'll borry them new fangled clippers the farm agent's got and it'll be a lot easier than cuttin' him."

"What kind of clippers is that, Papa?" Now I had something new to wonder about.

"I believe he called them 'maskalatomes. Says they'll do the job and never break the skin. Ought not to hurt too bad neither. Before ol' Billy knows what's happenin' to him we'll be done and there won't be a drop of blood to show for it."

Billy knew what was happening to him all right. He sensed it the minute Papa walked up to him and took him by the horns. It must have been something about Papa. Maybe it was in his voice. Or his eyes. Or maybe Billy just had a sixth sense that told him of the approach of doom. Anyway, he knew he was about to be deprived of something: his masculinity. And he was not about to submit willingly. So when Papa took hold on Billy's horns, Billy struggled with all his might, kicking, pawing and butting but Papa held on and wrestled him to the ground.

It was a noisy battle too, with Billy bleating and crying out in protest, and Papa trying to talk him down all the while. "Easy now boy" Papa said. "It ain't goin' to be all that bad. Here, Junior, hand me that rope and hold his hind legs while I tie him up. Don't let him kick you. Them hooves are sharp as razor blades and he'll cut you open with 'em if you ain't careful."

When Papa had Billy's feet all tied up he told Junior to get a good grip on the rope and hold tight. "You let him kick at the wrong time now and we'll have a devil of a time. Here Son," he turned to me. "You come and hold his horns and don't turn loose no matter what. You let him get loose and start in throwin' them horns around and we'll be in trouble."

I found myself looking directly into Billy's eyes and the tears were rolling down his cheeks as he uttered his cries of fear and despair. One anguished bleat as Papa closed the emasculatomes and quickly drew away. More tears rolled down Billy's cheeks as Papa untied the rope and set him free. Billy rose shakily to his feet and I stood facing him; the tears were rolling down my cheeks too.

"You think he's hurt, Papa?" I asked. "You think Billy's hurt bad?"

"He's hurt all right, Son. He's hurt in ways I can't tell you. His pride's hurt Son." Papa's voice sounded like there were tears in it too. "A goat's got a lot of pride. And we done something to him today he ain't never goin' to git over. But maybe we can live with'im now. He won't give off that God-awful scent. Only thing is, I don't know whether he can live with us after what we done to him...Come to think of it, I might have a bad time livin ' with myself for a while if I let myself think about it... Now you boys run to the well and git a bucket of fresh water and bring it here to Billy."

From One Eighth To One Sixteenth

Jeb Turner owned two hundred acres of good farm land in Green County Kentucky when the Ace Gas people began drilling in the area. The drillers soon found natural gas on a half dozen farms in the county. But when the representative for Ace Gas came to talk with Jeb about drilling for gas on his farm Jeb's response was not at all encouraging. Not even friendly. , Definitely unfriendly.

"There ain't nobody gonna drill no wells on my farm," Jeb asserted. His lantern jaws were set firmly over ill fitting false teeth.

"I heired this place from my ol' Daddy and he heired it from his Daddy who was my Gran'daddy and I can remember when I was just a boy in knee britches hearing my or' Gran'daddy say that God created the land for a man to farm and raise crops on and not for him to go a gold diggin' in."

Jeb's response to the Ace Gas representative was tinged with anger. That anybody would propose to tear up his land and dig holes in it in search of gas which God had put there and covered up to keep man from getting his greedy hands on it was an insult to Jeb's dignity.

He was tempted to tell the young fellow to get off his place and stay off but he contented himself with the acid remark about gold digging.

Jeb's wife Lucy would have liked to have some of the things that gold - in the form of natural gas in this case - would buy. Like modern appliances for the kitchen and some new furniture. Even a late model automobile. But she kept quiet because she could see the state of mind that Jeb was in and she went about her work in the kitchen.

"Oh I would love to have a modern kitchen range more than anything in this world," Lucy remarked to her daughter Sarah Beth. "But your Pap says he won 't go in debt for frivolous gadgets and I reckon that's that."

Jeb had often stated his policy on economics. "I own this land debt free and the quickest way I know for a man to lose what he's got is to go in debt for what he can do without."

But then the Ace Gas people sank a well on Abner Hatfield's place which lies to the East of Jeb's farm. The well was about three hundred feet over the boundary line and they set up a little pump to pump the gas, which it did night and day without anybody having to stand over it and watch it. Jeb and Lucy could hear it out there whacking and clacking away, and when Jeb went to plow his corn and sucker his tobacco he could see that pump going up and down "Like there's an invisible man there punpin' and he don't never git tired or hafta quit to go to dinner,"

It wasn't a long time, not more than the time it took for Abner to cash his first check, before Jeb saw something else. He saw a brand new Buick standing on Abner Hatfield's driveway.

Jeb did not mention Abner's new Buick to Lucy because he remembered that Lucy had mentioned the age and state of disrepair of the Dodge they drove to town on Saturdays, to church on Sundays, and once in a while to visit relatives as far away as Campbellesville. Like on Thanksgiving or Christmas. And remembering, Jeb thought it best not to mention Abner's new Buick. But Lucy noticed it anyway.

The first day she noticed the new Buick she jumped to the wrong conclusion- "I see that Abner and Mary have company. I wonder who could be visiting them in the middle of the week."

It was not unusual for rich relatives from town to visit a farm family on Sunday and be rewarded for their condescension with a carload of garden produce. But in the middle of the week? And besides, the car didn't leave after a decent interval. It just stayed on and on and on.

But nobody would stay on and on and on without ever being seen by a close neighbor. And besides, whenever the Buick did move off the driveway Abner himself was at the wheel, and Mary was "sitting up there beside him like the Queen of Sheba."

Lucy said to Jeb "I reckon they must've bought it with gas

money. A pity we don't have gas on our place."

Jeb had never said there was no gas on the Turner place. Just that he didn't want the drillers coming in there digging holes and interfering with his farming operations- Lucy noticed, and actually called attention to the fact, that Abner's gas well was pumping away right in the middle of his corn field. But she was careful to say this in a manner that would not reflect on Jeb's good judgment.

A few weeks after the Buick appeared on the Hatfield driveway the Ace Gas people sank a well on Timothy Oldham's farm which bounded Jeb Turner on the West. The first well didn't produce anything and Jeb commented to Lucy that Timothy had let those people come in there and tear up his place for nothing. But then the Ace Gas people tried again and this time "right smack dab in the middle of Timothy's tobacco patch" and just a short distance from the boundary with Jeb's farm. It was a big producer and Timothy was so elated that he bought a new tractor to celebrate.

Timothy's new tractor had an enclosed cab with air conditioning and a radio. The instrument panel looked like a jet airplane's and a man could sit up there and operate it with his good clothes on without getting dirty if he was of a mind to do it. The reason Jeb knew this was that Timothy was so proud of his new tractor that he called over to Jeb who was out walking over the farm and invited him to come across the fence and look at it. Even to climb up into the cab and get the feel of it.

"Must've cost a pretty penny," Jeb observed, visibly impressed by the luxury and efficiency of the machine.

Timothy nodded his head but didn't seem to be concerned about the cost of his new tractor. "Lots of pretty pennies in that little hole in the ground out there." He nodded toward the mechanical pump whacking away in the middle of his tobacco patch.

They stood there watching the pump for a minute or two and Timothy said "Might be gas on your place too Jeb. A feller never knows what's under his feet till he digs. "Jeb didn't reply and Timothy added "The Good Lord put some good things for us under the ground as well as on top. It might just be His way of tellin' us to dig for 'em."

Jeb Turner completed his walk, surveying the land with an

eye to the elevation, and for the first time he noticed with concern that his land was at a slightly higher elevation than the Hatfield and Oldham farms. He became pretty deeply concerned, even disturbed by what he saw and he reasoned within his own mind: The gas is on my place and it is flowing downhill to Hatfield on the East and Oldham on the West and they're tapping and selling it and getting rich offa me."

When Jeb came home Lucy noticed that his face registered some deep concern and she asked him if something had gone wrong. She thought the cows might have broken through the fence and got into the corn. But Jeb didn't really look like a man who had been chasing cows. He looked more like a man who was deep in thought and his thoughts were not the kind of thoughts that make a man happy and improve his appetite. Jeb had hardly touched his dinner - that is the noon day meal on the farm and this was not at all like Jeb to just pick at his dinner. He was normally a hearty eater, especially when he had been out on the farm all morning.

She knew it was not the food because she had made fresh corn bread to go with the green beans and sweet corn and Jeb liked nothing better than fresh corn bread with green beans and sweet corn from the garden, with a few strips of bacon cooked with the green beans to give them a little flavor. But Jeb wasn't interested in his food.

Lucy didn't say anything more about it . She just waited and when she started to clear away the dishes from the dinner table Jeb said "Abner Hatfield and Timothy Oldham are drainin' the gas off this place and sellin' it and gittin' rich."

"Oh My!" Lucy exclaimed. "How are they doing that?" Then Jeb explained to her how the land lay and how the gas was flowing out from under his farm to the Hatfield farm on the East and the Oldham farm on the West and how he was being robbed of what was rightfully his.

Then Lucy decided that she had to speak her piece no matter what and she said "Ain't no way for you to fight it Jeb, but to trap the gas here before it reaches them."

This was exactly what Jeb was hoping she would say because it was what he had already decided to do but he dreaded that she would throw up to him what he had said about not letting the Ace Gas people drill for gas on his land. Now he said to her "Get

me the card that Ace Gas feller left here with his name and telephone number on it."

Mike Renfro was young, brash and ambitious. He was young
enough to set the value of natural gas above the farm land that
covered it. Brash enough to give his card to Jeb Turner when that
irate land owner had stopped just short of ordering him off the
farm. And ambitious to make his first million before he reached
his thirtieth birthday. If he could buy up enough gas leases on
the farms of Green County, and the wells came through with
enough gas, Mike Renfro would achieve that goal. He was very
near it when Jeb Turner called and told him that he was ready to
talk with him.

They sat on the shady porch of Jeb Turner's farm house and
Mike had confidently assured Jeb that the damage to his fields
would be minimal and temporary and that drawing off the gas
would not affect the productivity of the soil above it when it was
replanted and cultivated once they had installed the pumps and
the pipes.

"Any more questions?" Mike asked, for he was still brash
enough to believe that he could answer any question the farmer
might ask.

"Just one," Jeb replied.

"What is it? Fire away!"

"What part do I get of the money the gas brings?"

"One eighth."

"One eighth?!" Jeb Turner's eyebrows shot up and his voice
rose almost a whole octave as he exclaimed "One Eighth!"

"That's what your neighbors Hatfield and Oldham get. One
eighth."

"That may be enough for them," Jeb Turner said, his voice
dropping to a low growl. "But I'm holdin' out for one sixteenth."

Dude McGraw Meets
His Match

Dude McGraw was the biggest boy in the Cane Bottom Grammar School. Not the brightest. Just the biggest. He was fifteen years old and weighed two hundred and ten pounds.

Dude was carrying enough fat around the middle to give the impression of wearing an automobile tire for a belt. And to produce a waddling gait when he walked. If it is possible to waddle and strut at the same timer Dude had achieved that too. In his own mind, Dude was the King of the Mountain. He had enough fat in his head to account for this misconception And to produce an unpleasant effect on others when he talked, as well as when he walked. It was his great size that enabled Dude to dominate the school yard. Because he was bigger than anybody else in the Cane Bottom Grammar School he was able to reign as King of the Mountain.

As a topographical fact, there was no mountain near the Cane Bottom Grammar School. The school was located in the Jackson Purchase Area of Western Kentucky, where the Land is so flat that it is not a very great leap, or fall, from the heights to the bottoms.

But this story is not about mountains and flat lands; it is about the encounter between Dude McGraw, who considered himself the King of the Mountain, or if the reader wishes to supply a more topographically correct term, Lord of the Bottoms, and Miss Audie Murphy who was the biggest school teacher the Cane Bottom Grammar School had ever seen.

Miss Audie, since we are introducing the combatants as they stand in their respective corners, weighed one hundred and eighty pounds. None of it was fat, and a large part of it was brain. And heart, or courage, the two being the same equipment for effective combat. And Miss Audie's gait, or movement, unlike Dude's, was more like a battleship under full sail, or steam. And in keeping with this image of a ship of the first line of the fleet, Miss Audie was without frills or folderol.

She wore no jewelry. She stood six feet in her low heel shoes. She wore her hair done up in a no nonsense bun on the back of her head. Miss Audie was ample in bust, which is to say that she made an imposing entrance, whether it was to her simply furnished classroom at the Cane Bottom Grammar School or to the more decorously appointed Cruikshank sitting room. Mister Hershel Cruickshank was Chairman of the School Board.

Miss Audie's appearance bore one noticeable abnormality. One cold blue eye was cocked up in such a manner that she seemed to be perpetually staring down in Jovian displeasure from the height of that elevated left eye. As cold and blue as the North Atlantic, that elevated left eye served as an aid and adjunct to the commanding countenance of Miss Audie Murphy. And if Dude McGraw had possessed more brains and loss fat between his widely flaring ears, he might have avoided the conflict which he in fact precipitated.

This unwise move on Dude's part may be understood if not excused though in the light of past performances- For he had run off Miss Audie's two immediate predecessors and he quite naturally assumed that he would run Miss Audie off too.

The first to be run off by Dude McGraw was Miss Rosie Timmins, fresh out of school and on her first teaching assignment. Dude, eager to gain the ascendancy, sassed Miss Timmins and made inappropriate remarks about her physiological equipment. Then he followed up these remarks with an attempt to kiss her in front of the whole school. Miss Timmins was both agile and strong. She was able to repulse him but she was quite upset by the experience. Consequently, she resigned, saying that she would not be slobbered over by that big ape in order to hold the school teaching job.

She demanded, and got, her full year's salary of six hundred dollars, although there were still three months left in the contract period. Mister Hershel Cruickshank felt that what had happened in Miss Timmins' classroom was a disgrace and they wished to avoid the scandal which Miss Timmins threatened to bring upon the community by initiating a law suit against the School Board and the parents of Dude McGraw.

After a short lapse of time the School Board employed Mister James Abercrombie as teacher for the Cane Bottom Grammar School. Mister Abercrombie was a slightly built and somewhat effeminate young man whose voice had not undergone the normal change. He had some experience in his profession but none to qualify him to cope with Dude McGraw who bullied him unmercifully and finally beat him up in the school yard. This latter incident took place because Dude was in the act of appropriating the lunch of a much smaller boy. Mister Abercrombie attempted to dissuade Dude by telling him that he was not acting in a gentlemanly manner. Dude, lacking any knowledge of the manner in which gentlemen are expected to behave when they are hungry and are tempted by food in the hands of a smaller person, gave Mister Abercrombie a clout on the nose, bringing forth both blood and tears.

Mister Abercrombie departed that very night. He never even asked for the month's salary that was due him. Nobody in the Cane Bottom community ever saw him again. The School Board members made no effort to locate him for the purpose of forwarding payment for services rendered. They reasoned that they had Lost more on Miss Timmins than they had gained on Mister Abercrombie. Mister Cruikshank did have a man-to-man talk with Dude's father. "Your son is a element of discord in the school and we cannot continue to tolerate it. Unless something is done about it we will have to ask you to withdraw him from the school."

The elder McGraw replied that it was his right and duty to send the boy to school. "It is the teacher's duty to learn him something or know the reason why." Since both Miss Timmins and Mister Abercrombie had failed to "learn" Dude anything useful or socially uplifting, it must be assumed that both of them knew the reason why. When Miss Audie Murphy applied for the job, offering to finish out the unexpired term of her two predecessors the School Board members felt it was their duty to recite this bit of history to her, only slightly amended in transmission, the risk she was taking. so that she might know in advance

"Do you still want the school?" Mister Hershel Cruikshank asked, having prepared himself for her refusal-

Miss Audie replied "All I ask is that I be given a free hand . "

The School Board members readily consented to give Miss Audie a tree hand and she was given the job. On her first day in school she laid the orangewood paddle on her desk and called the school to order. She began to call the roll, requiring each child to stand and respond "Present" when his or her name was called. She had not yet reached the half way point in the roll call, which is to say that she had not yet called the name of Dude, or Doran McGraw, as she had determined his correct name to be, when a commotion broke out in the rear of the room.

Miss Audie paused in the calling of the roll She fixed her arched blue eye on the center of the commotion. That center was Dude, or Doran McGraw- He was showing something highly amusing to the other boys huddled about him, tittering and half-heartedly attempting to stifle their amusement at what ever it was that Dude was showing to them. One of the boys reached for Dude's object of interest and accidentally knocked it from Dude's hand. It fell on the floor, face up, and a chorus of shock and dismay went up from the younger, the feminine and the more respectful elements of the Cane Bottom Grammar School.

"Doran McGraw," Miss Audie spoke in a cold and commanding voice. "Pick that up and bring it here to me."

Dude held up a sheet of paper on which could be seen a nude drawing intended to be a representation of Miss Audie Murphy. Dude McGraw lacked the artistic giftedness of Gaugin, but he had produced a crude likeness which made his subject recognizable by his emphasis on the arched left eye, the stern straight mouth, and the prominent bust. He now came forward, grinning and smirking, and with an insolence expressed in bodily movements, he strutted to the front of the room, raking his hands on the desks of the other students as he progressed from the rear of the room to Miss Audie's desk, scattering their books, pencils and notepads on the floor in his wake.

When Dude reached the front of the room he extended his work of art toward Miss Audie, making certain that it was fully visible to all present. She ignored the drawing and caught his extended arm, bent it over his neck and locked her own left arm about his neck. Thus she drew him to herself in an embrace quite unlike that embrace in which he and Miss Timmins had been locked momentarily. It was such an embrace as enabled her to exert such pressure on his arm and neck as to lift his body to the tips of his toes.

With her right hand Miss Audie picked up the orangewood paddle from the top of her desk and applied it to Dude's backsides about forty times. Each blow became more forceful and more painful than the preceding one. The expression on Dude's face changed from insolence to surprise to incredulity to simpering submission. When she had finished this first phase of the learning process, she commanded Dude to retrieve the drawing from the floor where it had fallen when his fingers involuntarily opened with the first blow of the orangewood paddle.

"Pick it up," she ordered. "Tear it to shreds and dump it in the waste basket." Dude carried out this command with eager dispatch.

Perceiving that Dude McGraw was not a slow learner Miss Audie issued a whole set of instructions. "Return to your seat. Work the problems on pages thirty six through forty of your arithmetic workbook. Memorize pages eighteen through twenty in your Speller. When you have finished you will stand before the school and spell each word correctly in a clear and respectful voice. You will give me the answers to the arithmetic problems in the same manner."

On the next day Dude's Pa came to the Cane Bottom Grammar School to confront Miss Audie Murphy. He had received from Dude a slightly distorted account of the happenings. Pa McGraw felt that he was within his rights as a taxpayer, and doing his duty as a father to demand fair treatment for his son at the hands of the new school teacher- He had come determined to demand her apology for her unfair and uncalled for punishment of his son.

But when he found himself standing before Miss Audie's imposing and unflinching figure, and facing her cold blue eyes, one of which was arched and looking down upon him from Olympian heights, Mister McGraw changed his mind about what he would say. Instead, he announced that he had decided that Dude was now big enough, and had learned enough from his hooks, to go to work in the fields.

"The way I see it now," Hiram McGraw said to Miss Audie Murphy. "That boy ain't really cut out for learnin' and startin' tomorrow I'm puttin' him between the plow handles where he belongs."

Miss Audie told Mister McGraw that she thought he had made a wise decision. "Good Day, Mister McGraw," she added in dismissal. Then she turned back to her class where twelve boys and fourteen girls ranging from the first grade through the sixth waited for her in respectful silence.

Drying The Dishes And Other Chores Around The House

A STORY OF DOMESTIC RELATIONS

He was writing his epic myth of Apollo in modern dress and the Muses hovered about his head like butterflies on the flowers in the Elysian Fields. Apollo, god of Light and Truth, but untrammeled by the moral strait jacket of conventionality, loose in the world in modern form and creating a veritable hubbub of excitement among the religionists and the politically correct aspirants to high office! Apollo, whose wisdom wedded to that of Athena would set modern Man free to achieve his true godlike destiny in the twenty first century.!

He was himself caught up in dreams of attaining the heights of Olympos where his beloved Hero dwelt in divine light and immortal beauty. But he was struggling too in the turbulent waters of the Hellespont. For Olympos was shrouded in sea mist and he must catch more than a fleeting glimpse of the divinity if he would capture the mystery of god become man, of man become god, of avatar and apotheosis. Then the door flew open. She stood facing him in the open doorway, breaking his reverie and invading his holy of holies.

Her face, a classic patrician face softly molded by an overwhelming femininity, was not a pleasant face at that moment. She was angry. Harried. Her hair was shoved hack from her forehead where sweat was smeared by the hand that had done the shoving. Little beads of perspiration stood on her upper lip. When she spoke her voice was strident, her words were unwished for, her message unpleasant. "The dishes need drying," she said. "They're piling up so high I've no place to put them. And you are sitting here in your cave."

He stared back at her in amazement becoming alarm becoming anger. "The dishes? But can't you see I am writing? Can't you see...?"

It was an old bone of contention. Oscar fought for the ground where he stood to receive the inspiration from the gods who touch man's pen with fire. "Damn it all Ethel! Can't you let the dishes wait? What's so everlasting compelling about the damn' dishes?"

"And what's so compelling about your writing that you have to run as soon as you finish eating and leave me with the kitchen full of dirty dishes and pots and pans? The muse won't sit on your shoulder any other time? Only when there's dirty work to do? Common work! Work you're too good to do!"

It was true, up to a point. The point being Oscar's abhorrence of any form of manual or menial work. He wanted to spend his time from the moment he awakened in the morning to the time he fell asleep at night, reading, writing, talking about Ideas. He would have had all his meals in a restaurant.

"That would eliminate grocery shopping, cooking, washing dishes, and carrying out the garbage, all time wasting activities." He had said this to her more than once. She had memorized it and inside her head she spoke in reply.

"And you could sleep in your clothes at your desk. That would eliminate the need for changing and washing the sheets. Maybe even washing and drying your clothes!"

He saw himself moving inside a sealed, insulated tube of privacy, secure from the defiling effects of all the tasks he hated. "Drying dishes indeed! Is there a divine mandate written in stone, requiring Man to wash and dry dishes immediately upon rising from the table? Or if you MUST wash them, are you afraid they will take wing and fly away if I don't come and dry them at the very moment you decree it? What's wrong with letting them drain dry!?"

Ethel saw this as a personal putdown. "Oh you think you are too GOOD to do the menial tasks!" As a withdrawal from her. "The dishes are for common people whose feet touch the earth when they walk!" He was just plain lazy. "Maybe you would just like to swap places with me. Yes, beginning tomorrow YOU can do the cooking and dishwashing. And the vacuuming of the floors. and washing and. drying the clothes. And making the bed. I have other things to do with my time too. You will see!"

All these threats rolled off Oscar like the proverbial water off a duck's back. He'd heard it all before. Time and time again. A tirade of this nature once a month. He could time it by the changes of the moon. But wait a minute. There was something new this time. SHE HAS SOMETHING ELSE UP HER SLEEVE! What did Ethel have in mind? What was Oscar going to see? She was secretive about it. Oh, she went on cooking, washing the dishes, churning up a storm with the vacuum cleaner, running the washer and dryer until every thread of their clothing had felt the cleansing power. But she was a quiet one. A deep one. Oscar could see that she was DOING SOMETHING. She had a PRO-JECT. A PLAN OF ACTION. Ethel had something going on inside that curly blond head of hers. Something to match his own absorption with his books.

Something to outdo his daily visits to the coffee shop. The unveiling would not come at his bidding though. It would be when Ethel was ready. IN HER OWN GOOD TIME. HE WOULD SEE!

The hour came. She told Oscar "I have joined an investment club."

"An investment club? My God! What do you know about investments? You're going to lose your ass!"

"Don't be crude. Besides, it's my ass. You're sitting on yours. But you just go on with your visits to the coffee shop. Lock yourself up in your den. Lose yourself in your papers and manuscripts. I am building a future."

"Future! My God! We're in our future. The future came for us when we retired. We're..."

"For you, maybe. Not for me. Oh, I know you say you retired to write. But what has it got you? What have you published? Who's paid you a dime for anything you're writing? When are you even going to recover mailing costs on all that junk you're putting out?"

"Junk, is it? It's my life. My raison d'etre. It's what's keeping me out of the loony bin."

"Keeping you out? Are you sure you've not been in the loony bin all along? Wrapped up in your dreams, your myths, your fantasies, your fairy tales and phantasmagoria!"

He didn't realize she knew the word phantasmagoria. Besides, his anger about being under attack was blunted by the reference to a secret weapon in her arsenal. It was now becoming evident that her involvement in an Investment Club could he more destructive than the atom bomb. He glared at her. "But you Ethel, you're going to sink everything in some fool investment. We'll wind up in the poorhouse. Talk about postage! We won't he able to buy stamps to write for help from friends."

Ethel proved to be more canny than Oscar thought. She had got all the condensed wisdom of the experts in written form. She had checked carefully the track record of every stock she was interested in. She was going about it carefully, cautiously and already her five shares in Amalgamated Steel had gone up seven points. And she had served TV dinners four times in a week.

Oscar hadn't noticed the TV dinners. He had sold a story. To a little magazine. And it wouldn't come out until next spring. "But it's a start!" he exulted. "Just what I need. Some name recognition . To be able to list some publications in my bio. You'll see. I'm on my way!"

Ethel sees. She has noticed that Oscar is standing beside her at the kitchen sink after dinner. Dish towel in hand. The Muses are waiting.

A Big Family Get Together

"Now you remember Oscar, the family reunion at Oak Grove is November the seventeenth. That's just three weeks from now." Ethel was studying the calendar hanging on the wall over the telephone. She circled the seventeenth of November. "That's on Sunday" she added, drawing the circle darker and darker.

"Appropriately so," Oscar replied. "Ancestor worship should be practiced on a holy day. The food offerings might be rejected if the annual rites are performed on a mere week day."

"Don't start in making derogatory remarks about my family, Oscar. They may not have any interest in your intellectual pursuits but members of my family love and respect one another."

"I know. I know. And they are so numerous that means their love is damn near universal." Oscar was working with a problem of cosmology. He was trying to harmonize the Greek concept of Hades with the Judaeo-Christian beliefs which had blossomed into a doctrine of a flaming hell. He was also doing a comparative study of the Nordic god Wotan's Valhalla, the Greeks's Elysian Fields, and the Christian Heaven which he contended was often confused with the Islamic Paradise which differed mainly in that it promised much more attractive rewards in terms of pleasures that a man could appreciate- "Who wouldn't prefer a bevy of houris to playing a harp or polishing golden streets?"

Ethel glared at Oscar and informed him that her father, who had been a Methodist preacher, was a much more reliable guide in matters spiritual than his books of magic and mythology. "But you will be in for a big surprise!" she said. "You won't be required to take lessons in playing the harp and there won't be any golden streets for YOU to worry about."

"So what is expected of me at this big family get-together?" Oscar had drawn back from his cosmological speculations and was seriously considering a more earthly phenomenon. "Just what do I have to do besides sample everybody's deviled eggs and fried chicken?"

"You could try being civil to Harriett. There is no reason for you to make a point of snubbing her."

"Oh there is the best of reasons. Your Cousin Harriett has to give me her whole medical history, including the most recent cholesterol count. and I am NOT a medical doctor."

"She needs sympathy and you..."

"And you know where sympathy is to be found in the dictionary between...."

"Don't say it Oscar. I don't want to hear it again. Besides, this is a very special family re-union. We are celebrating Uncle Roy's and Aunt Bessie's golden wedding anniversary."

"Don't tell me those two old lovebirds have actually endured one another for fifty years. It's no wonder he wears a coat and hat all the time, to cover up the battle scars, more than likely."

"Well, if Uncle Roy has battle scars he wears them more graciously than you do yours. Besides, Bettylou and I have already talked about it and we think you ought to make the presentation speech because you are so good at talking and all."

"You and Bettylou eh? I can see you and your sister conspiring to make a fool of me. You will try to get me to make a flowery speech and then wind up looking like a fool because Uncle Roy and Aunt Bessie will look all around as if to see who I'm talking about."

"Well, if you want to make a fool of yourself it's up to you and you don't need any help. We just thought it would be nice if you would say a few words appropriate to the occasion."

"All right! All right! I won't be General Sherman. If I am elected I will serve even if I wind up with egg all over my vest. It's just that saying something nice about those two is going to endanger my immortal soul."

"HOW SO?"

"Well, don't the Scriptures say there will be no liars in heaven?"

".Oscar," There was a terrible note of finality in Ethel's voice. "You have three weeks in which to prepare a little speech to honor Uncle Roy's and Aunt Bessie's golden anniversary. If you can think up so many clever things to say in those stories you write surely you can do this for the sake of the family."

The three weeks passed, for Time's giant stride cannot be halted by him who dreads its arrival nor can it be hastened by the eager hearted. The seventeenth of November arrived for both Oscar and Ethel. On a Sunday, just as Ethel had said it would. She had baked a turkey and cooked beans and potatoes. She had baked bread and a cherry pie and she had brewed a half gallon of tea. It was all stowed in the luggage compartment of the car and then she thought to look around for Oscar but he had disappeared. She looked in his work room and in the wood shed and even went out to the garden but he was not there. She called but he did not answer and she said "I'll just have to go without him. But of all times!"

Then she heard the crunch of gravel on the driveway and Oscar's old pickup truck rolled to a stop amidst autumn leaves the wind had drifted. Ethel stood with her hands on her hips glaring at Oscar who announced in tones of righteousness "I've been to church."

"You've been to church." Her tone of voice implied that in doing so he had desecrated a holy place. "You haven't been to church in a month of Sundays and you pick THIS Sunday to go to church."

"I thought I might get some ideas about my speech at the family reunion. Where is a better place to do that than in church?"

"Well, I just hope you stayed awake. That would be something different for you. And that you won't garble what you heard from the pulpit." Ethel was still in what Oscar was wont to call "a snit" because things were not going smoothly for her on this big day when her family celebrated itself. "But let's be off. I don't want to be late."

It was a thirty minute drive to the little Oak Grove Baptist Church where the Baldwin family reunion was in progress. Ethel and Oscar were the last to arrive and several of the early arrivals commented on this but Oscar proudly announced that he had been to church. He said this in such a manner that it conveyed the superiority of a man's obligation to God over family ties. He added that the Reverend Thomas J. Walker had delivered a lively discourse on The Prodigal Son. "A damn' good sermon too " he remarked to a group of male Baldwins standing about waiting for the women to spread all the food on the tables set up in the little recreation hall adjacent to the house of worship at Oak Grove.

"First time I ever heard a preacher give any credit to that older boy who'd stayed home working and holding the farm together while that young profligate was off chasing skirts and throwing away his daddy's money."

A couple of the less well educated of Ethel's male relatives were not sure what a profligate is but it was evident to them from Oscar's tone that a profligate is not someone to be used as a role model for young boys.

At this point Uncle Roy and Aunt Bessie came out of a little room in the rear of the recreation hall. Bettylou had brought them to the church in her late model Buick and taken them to the little room to pin corsages of red roses on them and to touch up Aunt Bessie's face and straighten Uncle Roy's tie. Uncle Roy managed to appear surprised at the size of the crowd and just a bit confused by all the furor being made over them. Aunt Bessie appeared smug but pained lest anyone forget her suffering.

Both Uncle Roy and Aunt Bessie were dressed to the nines and Ethel nodded to Oscar; he came forward to face the well dressed pair and to hang a big blue ribbon with 50 printed on it about Uncle Roy's neck and then he presented a bouquet of yellow roses to Aunt Bessie.

"I have been asked to say a few words on this auspicious occasion," Oscar said. "And for once I am going to do what I was told to do: say a few words. Now having said my few words I would like to give Uncle Roy an opportunity to do the same, seeing as how it may be both his first chance and his last chance in these fifty years of connubial bliss. Uncle Roy would you like to say something to Aunt Bessie?"

Uncle Roy stared misty eyed all around the room, then reached over and touched Aunt Bessie on the arm to get her attention. He leaned slightly toward her and said "Bess, Old Girl, I'm awfully proud of you!"

But Aunt Bessie, whose hearing had gone bad on her in recent years, reacted with asperity to Uncle Roy's remark. She jerked her arm away from him and replied "Well, after fifty years I'd think so. I'm awful tired of you too!"

I Remember Miss Florrie

Miss Florrie was my teacher in grades five, six and seven. All three grades were in one classroom. Two rows of seats were assigned to each grade with the fifth grade next to the chalk board, the seventh grade next to the windows and the sixth grade sandwiched in between. We were all working on separate assignments and reciting at our own levels. It would seem that by the time I reached the seventh grade I would already know everything taught there but I didn't. There were even a few things taught at fifth grade level I still didn't know.

In addition to the three grades of instruction, Miss Florrie was principal of the school. It was called Colaparchee Grade School and there were two other teachers, one for grades one and two, the other for grades three and four. Miss Millie could charm the first and second grade youngsters into good behavior, but Miss Frances used a twelve inch ruler to paddle the hands of miscreants; she could bend a boy's hand back so far he would be screaming for mercy before he was hit. Serious infractions of school rules meant being sent to Miss Florrie who kept the Orange Wood Paddle in the top drawer of her desk. The OWP was standard instructional equipment for the upper grades but I was still in the fourth grade when I got into the egg throwing escapade with two upper classmen. These two who led me astray were my brother Junior, and the school's most notorious bad boy, Ace.

We found the hen's nest in the blackberry vines on the edge of the school yard one Sunday afternoon. The eggs were well along the way toward the stage at which eggs should be strictly avoided. Ace had a very inventive mind. "Let's throw them at the school house door," he suggested. Some sailed high and broke on the arched window over the door, then slid down over the door and lay puddled on the floor.

On Monday morning Miss Florrie discovered our crime and set about the discovery of the criminals. Nobody would confess when she lined us up on the school grounds facing the area of devastation. She then gave us all the smell test, sniffing our clothes, our hands and our hair. We had not only thrown the eggs at the school house door but had also had a battle royal, with eggs breaking over heads and bodies. This was Sunday afternoon, as I have mentioned earlier, and we'd had our weekly baths on Saturday night, so the odor of rotten eggs lingered about us. Miss Florrie quickly came up with the three culprits and forthwith applied the Orange Wood Paddle to our backsides, much to our beneficial instruction in social behavior. Mine anyway. I cannot speak for Ace because he was reputed to be incorrigible and I will not speak for Junior because he is my brother.

After the egg incident I spent three years struggling with arithmetic under Miss Florrie's tutelage. The other subjects never gave me much trouble, to my knowledge, but the Tables did, especially long division. It may be that I became so hung up on long division that I didn't realize I was deficient in language skills. Or maybe Miss Florrie was just saving that little discovery for my fourth year. No, I didn't fail the seventh grade but when I graduated from grade school and was all set to ride the school bus into town to attend Lanier High School for Boys Miss Florrie made known her misgivings about me to my parents. She told them I was not ready.

I do not know whether she admitted that any of the fault lay with her teaching. I think she just told them I had not learned all I needed to know and she was concerned lest I get up there to that big high school in Ochmulgee, a school named for Sidney Lanier, Georgia's Poet Laureate of Song of the Chattahoochee fame, and I wouldn't even know my tables. So how on earth would I ever learn Algebra unless she gave me another year of special instruction on an individual basis.

She proposed to do this by taking me out of the home environment which seemed friendly to my continuing in ignorance, into her own home where she could watch, guide and direct my every movement toward the goal of becoming an educated man.

Miss Florrie had three boys of her own, plus some nephews whom she greatly favored. They had all gone off to college that year though, and Miss Florrie was left alone without a boy in the house. She thought I would fill an empty spot there, so it would be a mutual benefit deal.

My parents were firm believers in the work ethic; Miss Florrie made the trade more attractive by telling them I would have daily chores in addition to my studies. I would bring in coal and kindling for the fires I would build morning and evening; I would carry water from the spring; and I would gather the eggs. My father believed that too much reading, to the neglect of manual work, would result in a warped personality; Papa readily agreed to Miss Florrie's proposal. My education had begun.

Miss Florrie had rightly divined that I had no future in the mathematical sciences; she steered me rather forcefully in the direction of language skills. "You are going to do your work with words," she said, for at that time I had heard the call to preach, "and it is very important that you use the right words and that you use them properly." That was a foreshadowing of what was to follow.

My first decision regarding my studies at Lanier High School was whether to study Latin. I was against it, being of the opinion that Latin is a dead language and would be of no use to me. "You WILL learn Latin." Miss Florrie said. "It will help you to know what you are saying when you speak English." I had not thought of that. Miss Florrie knew her Latin but during the three years I was in her class room I'd never heard her say a word of Latin, not even the opening words of Julius Caesar's account of the Gallic Wars. But she could say what she wanted to say in English and nobody had any trouble understanding what she meant. Besides, the OWP was always there to further elucidate her words if a student was slow of understanding.

When the Latin command had soaked in - there was no question whether it would be obeyed - she dropped the other shoe. "Greek" she said. "You will study Greek too when you get to college." I hadn't even thought about college. I was still thinking about the eighth grade at Lanier and five years of ROTC with the drill sergeant barking at me in military-ese. But I settled into conjugating Latin verbs and declining Latin nouns; then I discovered the hidden barb in Miss Florrie's statement about using the right word in the right place and in the right manner.

Mama had always frowned on such linguistic abuses as "ain't" and "naw" as the corruption of "no." Besides, nobody said "I ain't" to Papa when he assigned a task, and it was always "Yes Sir" anyway. But I was guilty of handling syntax loosely and of committing grammatical faults with impunity until I went to live with Miss Florrie.

She laid out the rules of the game and the parameters of the playing field very simply. "I have taught you the rules of grammar. You know better than you are doing. Now, whenever you use a word improperly I will correct you. No matter where we are, when it occurs, and who else is present to hear us when I do it."

I didn't believe her. Nobody would do a thing like that to a thirteen year old boy. It would be embarrassing. Even humiliating. Downright damaging to the ego, as well as to the boy's self esteem.

I was wrong; she did it. But I was right too; it was humiliating. It occurred at a family dinner. Her family, which was rather large and had as one of its esteemed members Miss Millie, a younger sister of Miss Florrie. She had taught first and second grades. Here I was a freshman in high school and making language blunders like a first grader. Shame! I didn't do many repeats.

Miss Florrie thought I should not only "say it right" but say it without the aid of written or printed material in hand. "If you can't remember what you want to say long enough to say it, how do you expect your listeners to remember it long enough to do something about it?"

She had based this argument on the presumption that other people would want to "do something about " the things I said. That has not been borne out by my experience. It may be a good thing too. Once while I was in theological school, where I had finally got around to studying Greek and even a little Hebrew too, I memorized John Calvin's Institutes but then I never found them to be of any use to me afterwards; the only thing I did about Calvin's Institutes was forget them.

Miss Florrie seemed to take it personally when I answered a question by saying "I don't know anything about that." After all, I had sat in her classes for three years and had slept under her roof for as many months and I ought to know SOMETHING about ANYTHING that a reasonable person would ask me about. So when she asked me if I would like to go with her to see the movie MUTINY ON THE BOUNTY. and I said I didn't know anything about it, Miss Florrie became downright didactic about MUTINY ON THE BOUNTY. Using the Socratic method of teaching, she began questioning me on the subject.

"What is a mutiny?"

This was going to require great care in answering. I had to give the right answer, using the right words in the right relationships- "A mutiny is a rebellion of some sort." I was beginning to feel a bit mutinous myself.

"Military or civilian?"

"Military, I think."

"You know. What branch of the military?"

"The navy."

"Where did this naval insurrection take place?"

"On the Bounty."

"What was the Bounty?"

"A ship, I reckon."

"YOU reckon?"

"A ship."

"Whose ship?"

I didn't know. I really didn't. I made a guess, hedging my bet. "Ours. Or England's?"

"Which? "

I guessed again. If it was ours I should have heard about it. "England's."

We climbed into Miss Florrie's Dodge coupe and drove to the Rialto theatre in Ocmulgee to see MUTINY ON THE BOUNTY. I hated Captain Bligh; I hoped John Adams would not hang for his crime. I wanted him and the whole mutinous crew to stay on Pitcairn Island eating breadfruit and making love to the beautiful girls there. John Adams stayed long enough to make a lot of little Adamses but Miss Florrie did not encourage a discussion of that part of the story. She had her own personal reason for staying clear of matters having to do with romantic attachments between men and women.

Miss Florrie had a tragedy in her life related to marriage. Her husband had disappeared, leaving her with three small boys to raise without his help. Nobody knew what had become of him.

Nobody dared to ask. Was he dead or alive? Were they divorced? Did they quarrel and split? Or did he quietly slip away under the cover of darkness to recline in the arms of some voluptuous woman who was less demanding upon his use of the English language? Had she ever heard from him after he left? If anybody asked these questions, he didn't ask the only person who knew the answers to them. If the matter was discussed at all, it must have been within the family circle; nobody brought up Miss Florrie's erstwhile husband at the family gatherings I attended. After we had viewed MUTINY ON THE BOUNTY we talked about laws governing a ship at sea. We talked about the conditions on the ship which brought on the mutiny; we talked about what happened to the mutineers after Captain Bligh returned to England and reported the crime. We didn't talk about all the little Adamses procreated on Pitcairn Island because Adams and the others liked the beautiful young women there much better than they liked Captain Bligh.

I stayed with Miss Florrie that whole school term. The next summer Papa had work for me to do in addition to splitting kindling for Mama's wood burning cook stove, bringing buckets of water from the spring at the bottom of a steep hill, and gathering eggs from the hens' nests. Papa had serious work for me to do, chopping Johnson grass out of the corn field and picking cotton which I pushed into a croaker sack that I dragged along behind me. My parents didn't let me go back to Miss Florrie when September came around. Or Miss Florrie didn't ask to have me back because her boys were home from college. Or I didn't want to go back because I hated her boys; they were bigger than I was and they teased me unmercifully. I don't know the reason.

What I do know is that Miss Florrie had a profound effect on me. I now speak English.

Caleb's Body

At ten fifteen on Sunday morning the train pulled into Lewiston and came to a screeching, hissing stop beside the Central of Georgia loading platform. Martin Dean, agent for the Central of Georgia Railroad, peered through his bifocals at the bill of lading and motioned to the two young black men who stood to one side waiting for instructions.

"Rob Lee, you and Bubber come here with me."

They came hesitantly, rolling their eyes at one another. Neither of them spoke. "That's it," Martin Dean said. "Bring it out."

They had entered the railroad car but had not yet touched the crate. "Pick it up," Martin Dean said. "Don't just stand there."

They lifted the heavy crate, frowning and straining, and carried it to the platform. When they had set it down, they dusted their hands, as though they would dissociate themselves from further physical contact with the long bulky crate. They backed away to await further developments.

"All right Seeb." Martin Dean held out a slip of paper to a short black man who appeared to be about fifty years old. He was standing, hat in hand, at a respectful distance. "Sign your name right here."

The black man called Seeb was hesitant and Martin Dean said "Can you write?"

"Yassuh." Seeb did not accept the slip of paper. "Can I see 'im fust, Mister Dean?" Martin Dean looked at Seeb disapprovingly, as if he had been challenged.

"I mean...I wants to be sho' it's my boy, Mister Dean. They could a made a mistake, you know. Can I see 'im fust?"

"Well, I don't know about opening the box here." Martin Dean was thinking about the odor. "Well, maybe you're right. We better check. They might have sent the wrong one."

Under his breath Martin Dean said "They all look alike to me, but maybe not to his own daddy." He turned to Rob Lee and Bubber. "Go git a crowbar, boys and open the crate. We'll let Seeb be sure it's his boy. .. What did you say the boy's name was Seeb?"

"Caleb." Seeb wiped a tear away with the back of his hand. "Caleb's what me an' his Ma called 'im. It's a Bible name."

"Well, prize the lid up, Rob Lee. You and Bubber. Let's see if it's Caleb in there of if they've sent us somebody else by mistake. Prize it up." Martin Dean folded his arms across his middle and waited.

The nails in the packing crate made a scraunching sound as they were pulled out of the wood. "Pull that cover back from his face and let's see."

"Let Seeb pull it back." Rob Lee's eyes were wide and white. "I ain't wantin' to look."

"Go ahead Seeb. Raise the cover and see if it's Caleb."

Seeb pulled the covering back from the face. He stood for a long time looking at the face in the crate. His lips trembled and he wiped the back of his hand across his nose. It was dripping and his hand came away wet.

"Well, is it Caleb?" Martin Dean was impatient. "Is it your boy or not?"

"Yassuh. It's him all right, Mister Dean. It's Caleb."

"Well, sign the receipt and give me twenty three dollars and eighty five cents."

Martin Dean was extending the paper toward Seeb but Seeb drew back from it as if it were a snake. "Twenty three dollars and eighty five cents!? What for Mister Dean?" Seeb's voice rose almost to a screech as he turned to face the agent.

"The railroad don't haul people for nothin' Seeb. Not even if they're dead."

Seeb was trembling now and Martin Dean continued. "They sent him here from Detroit on the railroad. You got to pay the fare." He hated having to explain these elementary things to black people.

"But I ain't got that much money Mister Dean." Seeb looked back at the face in the box and walked away to the end of the platform. He took a small purse from his pocket and with his back turned to the group he started counting the contents of the purse. His lips moved as he counted.

Martin Dean spoke to Rob Lee and Bubber but without looking at them. "People ought to think about things like this before they go off and git theirselves killed." He glanced at his watch. "Church'll be startin' any minute now."

Rob Lee and Bubber made no response and Martin Dean did not expect them to. They stood back from the open crate, sullen and quiet. Rob Lee handed the crowbar to Bubber who began tossing it up and catching it. He missed and the crowbar clattered to the floor of the freight platform. Martin Dean stared at him disapprovingly and Bubber hastened to pick up the tool.

Seeb walked slowly back to the packing crate and looked in at Caleb. He stood for a long time, the tears flowing down his ebony cheeks. He tried to wipe the tears away with his fists. Then he began shaking his head; his lips trembled as he uttered unintelligible sounds; finally he muttered words as if speaking to the boy in the box. "I jes' ain't got it. I jes' ain't got it."

Then he turned and walked back to Martin Dean and repeated what he had said to Caleb. "I jes' ain't got it. I jes' ain't got no twenty three dollars and eighty five cents Mister Dean. You jes' gotta b'lieve me."

Rob Lee and Bubber were standing against the wall of the freight depot; they tried to make themselves invisible. Martin Dean looked severely at Seeb. "What do you mean tellin' me you ain't got it? You know you got to pay the freight on your boy's body. And here you are tellin' me you ain't got it to pay the freight on your boy after the railroad shipped him here from Detroit." Martin Dean stared hard at Seeb. "What are you gonna do about it?"

Seeb's lips trembled and he looked down at the floor of the loading platform. Rob Lee and Bubber tried even harder to make themselves invisible. Martin Dean looked at his watch and frowned. "I don' know, Mister Dean. I jes' ain't got it....I reckon you jes' hafta keep 'im. I reckon you jes' hafta keep my boy Caleb."

Seeb turned. His shoulders were bowed, his head down. He shuffled away. Rob Lee and Bubber pushed themselves even closer to the wall of the freight station, but there was a faint glow on their faces.

Martin Dean looked at his watch again. "It's church time." He started to walk away, paused, then started again and turned back. ""When I git back here from church I better not find no box on this platform. You hear me? Rob Lee? Bubber? You too Seeb. You hear me? All of you." He went down the steps, got into his Buick and drove away.

Come See What's Hanging
From The Family Tree

John A. Campbell was sitting with his feet up and minding his own business when the telephone rang. John's business was mainly that of finding a comfortable position in which he could read with a minimum of interruption and disturbance. The ringing of the telephone disturbed John A. Campbell because it interrupted what he was doing, reading. He got up out of his chair and answered the telephone.

"I am John A. Campbell calling from Kansas City," the voice on the telephone announced.

"No," John said. "I am not in Kansas City; I am in Ocmulgee Georgia."

"But that's why I am calling you," John A. Campbell in Kansas City said. "You see I am named John A. Campbell too and I am tracing the geneology of the Campbells and I want to talk to you and find out how you got to Georgia."

"I was born here," John A. Campbell of Ocmulgee Georgia said. He muttered to his wife Emily who wanted to know who was calling, "Some genealogy nut in Kansas City."

"Sorry," John A. Campbell in Kansas City said. "I'm a bit hard of hearing. What did you say?"

Emily frowned at John A. Campbell of Ocmulgee and indicated that he was being very rude to the caller. He said "I said the word is genealogy, not geneology." He spoke waspishly, for although he was not a genealogy nut, still, he was some kind of a nut; Emily said he was an extremist on words, their pronunciation and usage.

"Well, whatever," John A. of K.C. said, wishing to spread oil on the troubled Campbell waters. "I'm tracing the Campbell family tree."

"Found any horse thieves or bank robbers hanging from it yet?" John A. of Ocmulgee had decided to let the troubled waters flow over the dam; he would inject a bit of light humor into the conversation.

"No," John A. of K.C. said, trying to respond in kind. "But I haven't uncovered any millionaires either."

"That figures," John A. of Ocmulgee GA said. "Millionaires own horses and banks too."

"What does the A in your name stand for?" John A. of K.C. asked. Fearing he would not be clearly understood, he added "We both have the same middle initial. Don't you think that's unusual?"

"Yes, and it's the first letter in the alphabet. Easy to find."

"What's your middle name?" John A. of K.C. persisted.

"Alexander. MY father was a great admirer of Greek heroes."

"Was your father named Alexander?"

"No, he named me for Alexander the Great."

"Oh, John A. of K.C. said. He had not heard about Alexander the Great. My middle name is Adams; they named me for the President."

"Which one? Plain John or John Quincy?"

"The president." John A. of K.C. said, trying to be patient- "John Adams the president."

"Good, do you claim kin to him?"

"I'm working on that. There was an Adams in my mother's family way back about the time of the Civil War."

"I see. Was he married?"

John A. of GA was trying again for levity but it went over the head of John A. of K.C. who took a different line of attack. "How did your branch of the family come to be in Georgia?" John A. of K.C. had been trying to trace his own lineage back to the Mayflower and he had got as far as Virginia.

"They came over here with Oglethorpe."

"Oglethorpe! You don't say! What was he doing in Georgia"

"Building Savannah, I think. And figuring out ways to raise the taxes to pay for it."

"You don't say!" John A. of K.C. was not exactly a history buff in spite of his interest in genealogy. Oglethorpe's expedition had quite escaped his notice.

"Yes. and those fellows who had escaped the debtors' prisons in England were not too eager to go back in debt so they objected to paying high taxes."

"You don't say! How did they go about it?" John A. of K.C. had a personal reason for this question; he too objected to paying high taxes. He wanted to tell John A. of GA how high the taxes were in Kansas City but he passed in favor of finding out how the Campbells of Savannah got around paying high taxes.

"Well, the tax was based on the front footage of house lots in Savannah, so they built on very narrow lots and then went up a couple of floors to get the needed living room because they'd wound up with shotgun houses."

"You don't say!"

"Yes, and some of them even dug basements."

"How did that work out?"

"Not too good. The water got into them. Savannah is close to the water, you know."

If John A. of K.C. knew that Savannah was close to the water he hadn't thought about the effect on basements. So he said "Second and third floors! Boy! What a clever idea. How did that work out?"

"Not too good. Oglethorpe was clever too. He started taxing the second and third floors at the same rate as front footage."

"I'll be damned! What did he do about the basements?"

"Nothing. Said they could keep them for drowning rats in."

"Say, I'd like to drive down and have a real talk with you." John A. of K.C. added hopefully. "We might be kin."

"Drive carefully," John A. of GA said. "Yeah, be extra careful when you get to the city limits of Ocmulgee."

"Why?" John A. of K.C. now became cautious, wondering if the city streets of Ocmulgee Georgia were paved.

"I'd hate for you to get a ticket for speeding. They put stuff like that in the little newspaper here."

"You don't say!"

"Yeah. It's called the Ocmulgee Clarion."

"The Clarion, eh?"

"Yeah, I'd feel awful if I picked up the Clarion and saw that John A. Campbell had been arrested for exceeding our 25 mph speed limit."

Rabbit: A Story Of The South

Seeb pulled the soft, furry skin from the rabbit, turning it inside out as it peeled away from the still quivering flesh. A broad smile spread across his face as he contemplated the exposed, purplish meat, white streaked with fat. He whistled softly, happily, in anticipation of the feast. Wild meat was a rarity in the Springtime.

"Put the grease in the skillet ol' woman." Seeb turned large brown eyes toward the kitchen door. He was a big man, six feet tall, two hundred and forty pounds, most of it out front. Black. Very black. With great white teeth. All except the one gold tooth. Hattie Belle came into the open doorway; his rich laughter reached her, full of the conqueror's pleasure as he propped the gun against the corner of the wall. "We gonna eat young rabbit for dinner today. Praise God! Gonna have a real Sunday dinner."

Rabbit hunting on Sunday, even in season, and late Spring is not the hunting season, was frowned on in Ocmulgee Georgia. The Shiloh Baptist preacher did not like to have to compete with barking dogs, shouting men and booming shotguns when he opened the book to declare the Gospel. But Seeb had not gone hunting this rabbit on that Sunday morning in the Springtime; the rabbit came to Seeb.

Seeb was taking his rest, sitting in the back yard, leaning his chair against the wall of the unpainted pine weather board house, watching his garden grow. The rabbit just came slinking out of the weeds along the edge of the garden. Then he hopped over to the first row of collards and began nibbling the collard leaves. Seeb watched him for a minute without moving. He wanted to be sure the rabbit had come to stay. Then he eased the chair down, rose to his feet in a slow, gliding movement, and walked quietly into the house.

Hattie Belle looked up from her work in the kitchen; he motioned to her to be quiet. Thinking: Half grown rabbit. Ain't nuthin' better, he picked up his shot gun. Rummaging in a box that stood beside his bed, he found a shell, loaded the gun and stepped carefully through the doorway into the hack yard. The rabbit was still nibbling the young collard leaves, his nose twitching, his ears moving forward and backward to pick up any sound of danger. He paused and looked at Seeb but he did not run away into the weeds.

Seeb eased the gun to his shoulder when the rabbit went back to eating; he aimed carefully and fired. The blast of the shotgun broke the stillness of the Sunday morning like an explosion of ribald laughter in church.

The sound was heard far beyond Seeb's garden; it rolled out into the little run down section of Ocmulgee where the black people lived. The news of Seeb's action followed the sound of the blast; soon Seeb's neigbors knew he had shot a rabbit in the garden. Before the grease was hot in Hattie Belle's skillet the news was told and retold in the shanties farther down the dirt street. "Y'all heah a shot?"

"We heard. Who shootin'? Sound lak a shotgun!" "Seeb. He done shot a rabbit." The message soon reached Sim.

Sim was a small black man without pride or position even among his close neighbors. He had a lean and hungry look in his face and in his whole body. Sim lived alone in the shabbiest of the shanties at the far end of the street where the street itself petered out into a rutty country road. No woman would live with Sim for no woman wanted to listen to his whining, complaining voice all day long. He would be in the house all day because he wouldn't work, except on occasions of absolute necessity, when the rent of two dollars a month had to be paid. Then he did yard work for the white folks in Ocmulgee where he complained of hunger and got a handout from the kitchen. Other times Sim showed up at the houses of his black neighbors at meal times.

Sim's ears pricked up at the sound of Seeb's shot. His salivary glands responded instantly to the news that Seeb had shot a young rabbit in his collard row on the edge of his garden.

Hattie Belle dropped the rabbit, piece by piece, into the hot grease in the skillet; the still warm flesh cooked quickly to a golden brown. The grease popped and sizzled and the aroma of the cooking meat drifted through the open kitchen door and brought pleasure to Seeb's dilated nostrils where he sat in his chair, basking in the satisfaction of what he had done and in anticipation of what was to come of it. A good thing was being prepared for him in the kitchen. Then his pleasure was clouded by the long thin shadow of a visitor approaching the doorstep. It was Sim.

"Mawnin' Seeb." Sim assumed his most pitiable stance. "How y'all been lately?"

"We all right, I reckon, Sim. How you been?"

"Porely" Sim replied, his voice trembling. "It sho' hahd these days to stay alive. Ah goes hongry mosta the time. Awful hahd to git anuff to eat."

Seeb shifted in his chair and shifted his eyes toward the garden. Sim's eyes followed Seeb's. Young squash vines were blossoming bright yellow. Knee high stalks of corn held promise of things to come. The young rabbit had stopped short of Seeb's beans to nibble the collards. "Man doan' hafta go hongry if he got a mind to do a little diggin' in the earth. Good Lord give a harvest if a man do the plantin."

Seeb tilted his chair back against the wall of the house and waited for Sim's response to this suggestion that he work. Sim said "Ain't able to do no diggin'. My ol' back in such a bad shape. It hurt alla time."

Sim groaned as he sat down on the doorstep and reached behind him to rub his back with his hand. "Ain't gittin' no red meat to eat make a man's bones brittle. Ah gits up mawnin's Ah feel lak mah ol' back goan give out on me."

The thought came to Seeb's mind: Casting pearls before the swine. He said "Reckon a little red meat don't hurt nobody ef he c'n git it." The aroma of frying rabbit drifted through the doorway. Sim's nostrils dilated; his lips drooled. His eyes watered.

"Sumpthin' cookin' sho smell good" Sim said, straightening up. Seeb was quiet, looking out over the garden, wondering how he would get rid of Sim without having to share the rabbit with him. Hattie Belle came to the open doorway, saw Sim, and quietly closed the door. The odor of cooking meat died away on the warm air in the back yard. Sim became anxious.

"Ah heah y'all shot a rabbit this mawnin'." Sim resumed his starved look. "When y'all goan eat 'im?"

"Ah reckon we eat 'im sometime when we git ready. Ain't no hurry 'bout eatin' a li'l ol' rabbit."

"Ain't y'all gonna eat 'im fo' dinner?" Seeb's answer had deepened Sim's anxiety.

"Ain't no hurry, Sim, 'bout eatin' a li'l ol' rabbit. Me an' mah ol' woman we eat 'im one a these days when we git ready."

"Ah thought fo' a minit theah I smell rabbit fryin'."

"Collard greens, Sim. Collard greens," Seeb said. "You can't tell the diff'ence 'tween rabbit an' collard greens?"

"Ah sho thought I smell rabbit cookin'. Smell lak rabbit. Sho' as the worl'. Smell jest lak rabbit to me."

Hattie Belle opened the kitchen door and came out onto the narrow porch. The strong smell of collard greens came with her. "That you Sim?" she said. "Lordy, it sho' gits hot in theah cookin' collard greens. Seeb, you mind ef Ah sets in yo' chair a spell to cool off. Ah'll jest set an' tawk to Sim whiles you go git another chair. Ain't comf'table settin' on no do' step."

Seeb searched her face and found the barest trace of a sly grin there.

The grin was playing about the corners of her mouth; she wiped it away with her hand and there was grease on her fingers. "You find a comf'table cheer in the kitchen where Ah been cookin' them collard greens." She took Seeb's chair and sat down facing Sim.

"Ain't in the habit of totin' cheers f'r you ol' woman," Seeb said, but his voice was not as harsh as his words were. He went into the house and Hattie Belle settled herself heavily She began fanning with a folded newspaper and commenting on the hot weather so early in the summer. Sim showed little interest in the heat.

In the kitchen Seeb found the rabbit. Half of it, that is. He chuckled softly as he lifted the tasty brown meat to his lips. "Ol' woman done et her ha'f an' lef' me mine." He ate standing up. "Ah reckon ain't none f'r Sim. He goan hafta eat collards."

A few minutes later Seeb walked to the doorway, dragging a cane bottom chair . Outside, he set the chair against the wall of the house and leaned back contentedly. Almost without being conscious of his movement, he wiped his mouth with the back of his hand. "You sho' right 'bout it bein' hot in that kitchen, ol' woman." Seeb drew his hand across his sweaty brow. "Them collard greens sho' steam a place up sumpthin' awful." He glanced up at the sun which was now approaching the meridian. "Gittin' on t'wards dinner time too. You want to stay an' eat some collard greens, Sim?"

Sim saw the grease on the back of Seeb's hand; his hopes died. "Naw," he said. "Ah reckon Ah better git on home. Ain't et nuthin' but collard greens in a week. Ah's gittin' awful tard o' collard greens."

He rose from the doorstep and started off, mumbling "Man need some red meat, gamey meat to gi' 'im stren'th f'r hahd wo'k."

That Damned Computer

Oscar knew that Ethel had some big project brewing because she had been unusually edgy for two days, but he was on his search for the lost civilization of Atlantis, so she took him by surprise when she announced her intention to buy a computer.

He had considered the various possible locations where Atlantis might have slipped beneath the waves of the sea and he was about to settle upon the Mediterranean when Ethel said "I have to get the computer . We need it." Her statement seemed to imply that there had been considerable discussion of the subject. There had been no mention of a computer. Her tone indicated that she expected Oscar to oppose the purchase of a computer and he did.

Oscar recognized her statement as one of fixed purpose without touching upon the underlying reason, so his reaction was predictable. "And what in hell do we need a computer for?"

"Well, I have to keep track of my investments. I have to keep up with changes in the market as they take place. Reading about them in the newspaper the next day is not good enough."

The storm warnings were now flying. Oscar looked up from Graham Hancock's FINGERPRINTS OF THE GODS when Ethel said this. He placed his finger between the pages and glared at her. Now he laid a bookmark where his finger had been and prepared to do battle. "You're going to buy a computer to keep up with a forty nine dollar investment in the stock market?!" Then, to give the impression that the matter was settled in his favor, Oscar reopened FINGERPRINTS OF THE GODS and began considering the possibility that Atlantis sank off the horn of Africa.

"That was just the beginning," Ethel said. "I will he making investments on a regular basis. But to make wise investments I have to know what the market is doing, and on the Internet I can...." But Oscar had now closed the book and dropped it onto the table with a solid thump. Ethel came and stood over him. "Come out of the nineteenth century, Oscar. The mythological gods no longer rule the earth."

"Oh no. A giant computer is now located at the navel of the world. and it is in complete control. What I wonder is how it managed to get inside that head of yours which I have been unable to penetrate in the forty years...."

Ethel saw that it was time to shift the direction of this discussion. "The computer will be a big help to you with your writing, Oscar. It will save you a lot of time and make it easier for you to correct your spelling and grammar. You can just move a word or a sentence or even a whole chapter."

"Move sentences and chapters! My God! Do you suppose I don't put my sentences and chapters where they belong in the first place? And correct my spelling and grammar! Have you forgotten what Miss Florrie did to break me of using bad grammar?"

"I remember that you said she washed out your mouth with Octagon soap."

"That was for cussing. For bad grammar she corrected me in public until I was afraid to open my mouth. Do you think I am going to submit to the same form of abuse from a computer?"

"But think of the time you could save. And the gasoline. You drive up town every day to make copies. With the computer you could make your own copies as fast as you write."

Oscar thought about his daily visits to the Sunrise Cafe and coffee with his friends there. How would he justify all of that without the need to make copies. "Great! Now the computer is for me! You're going to save the time I spend with my friends and I suppose you'll have some little chores for me to do around the house with all that time I'll have on my hands since I won't be at the Sunrise. And we can stop worrying about the price of gasoline because I won't be burning any because I'll be sitting at home."

He knew he was mixing all the metaphors together into a string of oxymorons but he was desperate for a way out of the box Ethel was putting him in. So he went for the jugular. "Now

Ethel, suppose you just tell me how William Shakespeare ever managed to write Hamlet without a computer. And did Homer write the Iliad and the Odyssey on an Apple, or was it a Hewlett Packard? And Saint Paul. Did his computer plug into a wall socket in his Roman prison when he was writing half the New Testament? Come on Ethel. You have just made up your mind to play around with a computer and all these arguments you're putting up are nothing but...."

"You're right, Oscar. I'm going to have the computer. And I'm going to play around with it....In fact I have already picked it out at the computer store. Now. Do you want to go with me to bring it home, or do I have to ask Charles to do that too? He has already agreed to set it up for me and teach me how to use it."

Who is Charles?

Charles is a computer expert. He knows how to assemble all the component parts so that the speakers and the monitor and the microphone and the printer and the telephone and the keyboard will all be properly related to the computer brain and even an electrical surge will be no problem with Charles in command. Charles travels the Internet and he opens Windows 95. He downloads onto the hard disk and he plays games on the floppy disks. Charles smiles when Ethel asks questions. He looks benignly at Oscar from Olympian heights of omniscience but his handsome face is both serious and smiling and his clear blue eyes look into the inner workings of that mysterious monster overflowing the computer desk onto the floor and those same eyes look into the faces and the hearts of both Ethel and Oscar. And he works for free! Oh, a few meals, for Charles loves his Gran'ma's biscuits, and didn't Oscar take him along on the woodland trails even before Charles had started to school?

"Charles can even teach you to use the computer, Oscar!" But Charles must first teach Oscar to control the Mouse. For that Mouse is definitely the genius who controls the workings of the computer. Without the Mouse you cannot get into the computer and once in you cannot get out. Not without the Mouse!

"You just move him about, Gran'pa. Don't pick him up and examine him as if you are trying to find out what makes him work. Just click when the arrow points to what you want." Ah, but when Oscar moves the Mouse the arrow dances erratically among the images on the screen like a spaceship gone crazy among the stars and the planets in the heavens, what happens then?

Even the heavens are orderly though and eventually Oscar and Ethel become comfortable with the computer. Ethel was checking her latest purchase of Amalgamated Metals on the Internet and it seemed to her that she had made a wise choice. She was about to announce her gain to Oscar when the telephone rang and Oscar said "You answer it Ethel.! For he was deep into the evidence that Atlantis sank into the Aegean and he burrowed deeper into the mystery of that lost civilization, saying to Ethel "It will be your brother calling and wanting to know how much rain we got here last night."

Ethel lifted the receiver and listened. Oscar was almost certain now that it was either the Aegean or the Mediterranean when she said "it's for you Oscar. Some publisher in California. Says he has your manuscript called A HANDBOOK ON MARRIAGE, BOTH ANCIENT AND MODERN. He wants to talk with you about it. I didn't know you had written a handbook on marriage. You once told me the reason you don't spend time in research is that you only write about what you already know."

"Give me the phone Ethel!" Oscar snatched the telephone away from Ethel and said "Yes." In fact he kept on saying "Yes" to everything the California publisher said, and when he hung up Ethel looked at him with question marks in her eyes. "Putnam and Abercrombie," Oscar said. "A reputable publisher. Located on the West Coast."

Ethel's eyes continued to question him and he said "Mister Putnam says he is impressed with my grasp of the Greek myths and their absorption with the concept of marriage. Says he would like to change the title to THE MARRIAGE MYTH though and make a few other changes."

"A few other changes, eh! Well, I'm impressed with your grasp of the myths myself but when did you become an expert on marriage?"

"Oh it was while I was on the Odyssey with Homer." Oscar was feeling superior now and he could afford to be a bit condescending from his intellectual heights.

"THE MARRIAGE MYTH! Ha! Better call it THE MOUSE TRAP if you want to get the reader's attention." Ethel had turned back to the Internet, but Oscar was riding his Pegasus to riches and fame. He would have a best seller and his cronies at the Sunrise would banter him but they would know he had arrived too. He even became jocular , just thinking about all the things that would be said about him when THE MARRIAGE MYTH would be the talk of the town in Ocmulgee.

"Atlantis!" he said. "It must have been in the Pacific. Sank and rose again and attached itself to the continent. Now it's called Californis!"

The Hanging Tree

Ezekiel Hartshorne stood before the Honorable John Fortress, Circuit Judge of the Court in the little town of Ocmulgee and heard the Judge deliver the sentence. "I sentence you to be hanged by the neck until dead for the crime of murder of your wife Isabel on the twenty first day of June of this year of our Lord eighteen hundred and forty two."

A jury of twelve white men from the county of Colaparchee and the county seat town of Ocmulgee had found Ezekiel Hartshorne guilty of beating his wife to death with an axe handle.

Ezekiel had not denied that he had killed his wife. He had pleaded innocent of the charge of murder, claiming that his wife Isabel had been the cause of her own death in that she provoked him to the act by which she had died.

"She wouldn't let me rest, Your Honor." he argued in his own defense. "Night and day she nagged at me and there was no way of stopping her mouth but to stop it forever by an act in my own defense."

Nevertheless, the jury of twelve law abiding white men of substance and reputation in the community, men who attended church either regularly or occasionally, found Ezekiel guilty of murder in the first degree.

When Judge Fortress had pronounced the sentence, he harked back to ancient custom and said to the condemned man "Do you have one final request to make before I set the date and the hour of your execution?"

"I do, Your Honor," replied Ezekiel Hartshorne, and when the judge raised his eyebrows in expectation and as an invitation for him to speak and make known his request, Ezekiel said "I would like to choose the tree that I will be hanged on."

"That is an unusual request," His Honor observed. "Will you tell the Court why you want to choose the hanging tree?"

Then Ezekiel replied "Since this is to be my last act on this earth and I am never to see the light of day again when this act is done, I want to be hanged from a perfect tree in the hope that it may in some measure atone for my sinful life."

Judge Fortress smiled indulgently at what he considered a fanciful, perhaps even romantic notion based on the fear inspired by the harshness of the sentence which he himself had pronounced on this simple but sinful man from a one horse farm in the nearby countryside. What harm? he reasoned, could be done by granting this last request of a man condemned to die?

"The Court grants your request," Judge Fortress said, "And assigns Deputy Jake Winslow to accompany you as you go to select your hanging tree. And to insure the Court and the good people of the State of Georgia that you will not escape nor commit another crime while the search is underway. Make haste, and when you have found your tree, come back here with your neck ready for the rope."

Judge Fortress made this last word of instruction harsh and severe lest the condemned man be led to expect, or the onlookers in the courtroom suspect, leniency.

Ezekiel Hartshorne said "Thankee Judge," and turned to leave the courtroom in the custody of Sheriff's Deputy Jake Winslow. Since the day was far spent, the trial having taken up the most of it, Ezekiel was returned to his cell in the county jail where he spent the night brooding upon his sentence and planning where he would begin his search for the perfect tree. And, of course, reflecting upon his life with Isabel.

He was at that time sixty two years old. He had married at the tender age of twenty two, being greatly in love as he supposed because of the strong feelings of desire which he had for the fair Isabel, and he had spent forty years under the yoke of what those of a poetic mind may call connubial bliss. Ezekiel himself had defined the relationship, at least one side of it, his own, in his statement to the Court, that his wife of two score years had given him no rest by day nor by night.

****

"There is a big oak tree out at Midway that ought to be just right for your purpose," Deputy Jake said when he called for Ezekiel after breakfast the next morning.

Jake had rented a horse and buggy from the Ocmulgee Livery Stable and he was in what was, for Jake Winslow, a festive mood. He was by nature gloomy and suspicious of the criminal element but the novelty of this expedition had cheered him. The cost of the livery was being borne by the Court and that helped his spirits too.

"We will look at it," Ezekiel agreed, for there was nothing to lose. Not even time. For he could only gain time by looking. It was a morning's drive to Midway, and he already had a tree in mind down near the county line but he would not mention it to Jake at the moment lest it become a confusing element in the quest.

They drove out to Midway and Jake proudly pointed to his oak tree. It was a large tree, standing out by the road, casting its shade over the area directly under it for it was noon when they arrived. "Ain't no way a man could fault that there oak," Jake said. "She's strong enough to hang a mule team without bending a twig."

Ezekiel respectfully examined the tree from every angle. East. West, North and South. He even stood directly under it and looked up into its leafy branches. "The only angle he didn't look at it from," reported Jake when they returned to the jail that evening "was from above, and I swear before God there was a time there when I thought he would sprout wings and fly up in the sky and see how that oak tree looked from up there."

"It is one sided," was Ezekiel's verdict on the Midway oak.

And true enough, the tree was more heavily branched on the Southern exposure than on the Northern because it sought the sun. Heliotropic is the scientific term for this botanical condition. Ezekiel Hartshorne, being a simple, uneducated man, had no knowledge of the term. He had not even thought deeply on the fact that the earth, rotating on its axis, leans toward the sun, so that the shadow of a man, or of a tree, will be cast to the North and never to the South, and even on that one day in the year when the sun seems directly overhead at noon, the shadow will stand under a man, or a tree, but the next day it will begin to grow again to the North. And all the time the tree will reach toward the sun with the result that the branches and the foliage will be heavier on the South side.

But without having contemplated these scientific matters, Ezekiel Hartshorne knew that the Midway Oak was not a perfect tree because it was one sided. And that was enough to buy him one more day on the earth, one more day to see the light of the sun, one more day to live and to cheat the hangman's rope.

So they returned that evening to the jail in Ocmulgee. Jake returned the horse and buggy to the livery stable. "I'll need a fresh horse tomorrow," he told the hostler. "We're goin' to look at a tree down near the county line. One Zeke says he'd like to look at."

The hostler winked at the deputy and said "I've got a hoss that'll take you an' Zeke to the hangin' tree but you'll need a waggin' to bring 'im back to town in."

The deputy only frowned and made no reply. His business was to guard the prisoner while he found the tree; the hanging was another matter. He was not the hangman.

At sunup the next morning the deputy and his prisoner walked to the livery stable together. A chestnut gelding, already hitched to the buggy, showed the white of its left eye as it turned to examine them, raised one hind foot and stamped, trying to dislodge a fly. This failing, he swished his tail violently but this did not work either; the fly had found a place where he could not be reached and he proceeded to draw blood.

It was a pleasant fall morning and the gelding trotted at a leisurely pace under the occasional flick of the deputy's whip; they reached the chosen spot on the lower end of the county about noon and at a country crossroads store the deputy bought cheese and crackers and a can of Vienna sausages — this was at the Court's expense — and they ate in the shade of the overhanging roof on the porch to the store. The storekeeper was a bit nervous at first, finding himself host to a condemned murderer, but this soon changed, and he questioned Ezekiel about the judge's decree.

"What kind of a tree are ye a lookin' for?" The storekeeper had opened a can of sardines and was spearing them with the point of his knife blade and conveying them one by one to his mouth which opened under drooping mustaches to receive the small oily fishes. The sardines gave off an unmistakable odor and when the storekeeper belched the odor was carried a good distance. "What kind of a tree is it goin' to take for ye?" he repeated.

"Just a perfect tree," was all that Ezekiel would say.

When they reached the spot where the tree was standing, Ezekiel dismounted from the buggy. The deputy sheriff remained seated. "That 'un suit you?" Jake Winslow cut a plug of tobacco with his pocket knife, inserted the tobacco in his mouth and closed and returned the knife to his pocket.

Ezekiel made no reply. He walked around the tree, surveying it from every angle. At last, his eyes clouded with doubt, he returned to the buggy, put one foot on the hub of the wheel preparatory to mounting to his seat. "Limbs all grow up too straight," he said. "Rope'd slide down." He took his seat beside the deputy. "Won't do."

They started back to town and the gelding threw a shoe on his right forefoot, went lame and refused to pull the buggy at more than a three legged snail's pace. The storekeeper said "There's a blacksmith's shop down the road a piece."

When they reached the farrier's shop which consisted of a bellows, an anvil and a hammer under a shade tree, they had to wait in line. Ezekiel was undisturbed by this but Jake tried to use the leverage of office on the blacksmith.

"Can't help it if you are from the sheriff's," the man said. "Prisoners don't come ahead of reg'lar customers." The "reg'lar customers" were farmers with mules and a carter with heavy horses. Consequently, it was nearly sundown when the blacksmith raised the gelding's foot to look at it.

"This'll take some time," he said. "The hoof's damaged bad." The blacksmith was not entirely without humor or ingenuity. He glanced up into the branches of the oak that formed the roof over his shop. "You can use this tree if it suits you," he said, looking first at the prisoner and then the deputy.

Ezekiel spoke without hesitation. "Too close to the fire."

The deputy became anxious. "If we ain't back by dark, the sheriff will think my prisoner's escaped." He dispatched a boy on a pony to bear a message to the sheriff and gave the boy a quarter. "There's another quarter for you when you git back if you bring a note from the sheriff sayin' you told 'im."

That night they slept at the blacksmith's house. Jake Winslow handcuffed Ezekiel Hartshorne to his own wrist and they lay down together on a pallet the blacksmith's wife had made for them on the floor.

In the middle of the night Zeke shook the deputy and said "I hate to wake you up Jake but I have got to piss. Real bad."

****

The sheriff had become alarmed and was saddling his horse to go in search of the prisoner when the boy arrived on the pony with Jake's message. "It's a damn good thing you got here when you did," he told the boy. Then he wrote Jake Winslow a note and handed it to the boy who was already in the saddle. The note said "Check out all the trees between here and there on your way home tomorrow."

The deputy and his prisoner did that, the deputy discovering one likely hanging tree after another, and the prisoner finding some fault with each one.

"Too tall."

"Too low to the ground."

"It's wop-sided."

"Leans too much."

"Been struck by lightnin'. That's bad luck."

"How lucky can a man git at his hangin'?" the deputy snarled, growing impatient.

Ezekiel didn't answer. He squinted into the next tree and opined "Branches are too thick."

The search for the perfect hanging tree dragged on through the crisp and frosty days of Autumn. Even Jake Winslow began to notice the differences in trees. Some trees are heavily branched right down to the ground. A pine, or a spruce, if it grows out by itself in a field, getting the full sun. But if it grows in a thicket the lower limbs will die and drop off as the tree keeps forming new branches at the top. A pine tree eighty feet tall might not have a branch on it for forty or fifty feet from the ground. Who could get a hanging rope on a tree like that?

The large, strong limbs on a hickory are placed thirty feet or more up on the main trunk while the lower branches are small and weak and would bend under the weight of a man. And Ezekiel Hartshorne weighed two hundred and forty pounds; that is a considerable weight to suspend from a single rope looped over a tree limb.

Branches on an elm slant downward from the main stem and may even droop frivolously to the ground. The elm would certainly be inappropriate for use as a hanging tree.

Yellow poplar, sometimes called tulip poplar-scientific name, tulipifera liriodrendron, a combination of Latin and Greek-is brittle and might well break under the weight of two hundred and forty pounds, dropping the man to the ground, requiring a second hanging since Judge Fortress' sentence was that Ezekiel Hartshorne be hanged by the neck until dead.

Dogwood and sassafras were out by reason of their diminutive size and persimmon had no branches which Ezekiel considered adequate for his needs.

In fact, as the search for the perfect hanging tree dragged on from days to weeks and into the Christmas holiday' season Ezekiel's requirements became more demanding rather than less. Not only must the tree be fully capable of serving its grim purpose; it must look good, must be perfectly shaped with no deformities or irregularities. Three days before Christmas, High Sheriff Tom Watkins drew Deputy Jake Winslow aside and said to him "This is draggin' out too long and costin' the Court too much in addition to takin' you off the job here. I want you to find a hangin' tree and I want you to find it quick. I don't aim for the New Year to ketch me with this prisoner on my hands."

But Jake, who had come to feel a sense of camaraderie from being shackled to his prisoner for so many days and nights, said "Sheriff. It ain't for me to find the tree. You heard what Judge Fortress said."

Sheriff Watkins glared back at his deputy, vexed at a situation he had never faced before and Deputy Winslow added "Judge Fortress give that choice to the prisoner."

Nevertheless, the deputy and his prisoner went out again that very day to examine an oak in a grove ten miles from town. The tree was reputed to be a fine specimen and even Ezekiel would be hard put to fault it.

The weather was bad though. A cold. drizzling rain turned to sleet while they were inspecting the tree. Both men were soaked and freezing before they got back to town and Ezekiel had discovered that a dead limb had broken under the weight of water turned to ice, and so of course the tree would not do. When they arrived at the jail Ezekiel was shivering, his teeth rattled when he spoke, and his face was flushed. Soon thereafter he began to cough and he lay down on his cot in the jail cell but he could not rest. Jailer Harry Goodwin sent Deputy Jake Winslow out for some cough medicine, but by morning Ezekiel was worse.

The local physician, 01' Doc Powers, was summoned, and he listened to Ezekiel's chest and said "Pneumonia. Ain't nothin' I can do for 'im. I think he has cheated the hangman's rope."

On Christmas Day, Ezekiel Hartshorne died on the cot in his cell at the county jail. Jake Winslow was there when Zeke drew his last stertorous breath and when he had closed the prisoner's staring blue eyes he went to make his report to the high sheriff. "Sheriff," he said. "I have learned something which you can pass along to Judge Fortress if you are a mind to do it. After all, even judges don't know ever'thing."

"What is it?"

"Well, Sheriff, since I have been shackled to Zeke these past months I have learned that a tree is a heap like a man."

"Yeah? And how is that?"

"There ain't no perfect tree, Sheriff. Just as there a ain't no perfect man."

Down The Garden Path

It was an ordinary garden path. Beginning at the back door of the rustic brown cedar house among the trees, it wound through the azaleas and under the dogwood boughs and then past the fish pool and across the little wet weather rivulet where flat stones offered a dry crossing to the agile, and then ran quickly to her garden where veggies and flowers crowded together in a profusion of color and promise.

The path was only wide enough for one person to walk. If two walked holding hands or with arms embracing waists they could just stay on the outer edges. In dry weather she could avoid the early morning dew that lay on the grass on either side of the path. In wet weather the path was muddy though, but the good and the bad come together in such a garden path. Still, The path was a bone of contention between them.

She - that was Ethel - did not want any grass growing in the path. He - that was Oscar - disliked any bare spots, or streaks, in his grass covered landscape. Not even on the garden path. The garden was Ethel's garden, her retirement project. The lawn was his obsession.

"Obsession" was Ethel's term for the meticulous care which Oscar bestowed on his grass. "Mania" was the term Oscar applied to Ethel's savage attack upon any sprig of grass which dared to appear in her garden. Or even on the garden path. "Ethel hates grass like the devil hates holy water" Oscar had been heard to say.

"Heard it a million times" was Ethel's response. "Oscar thinks there is a hidden eleventh commandment Thou shalt not cut the grass shorter than four inches."

That was another bone of contention. Ethel said "'It's like

wading through a hay field." But Oscar was adamant in his insistence that the grass should not be cut short because that robs it of the foliage necessary to gather nutrients from the air. "Tall healthy grass keeps down noxious weeds and stands up better in hot dry weather."

"Stand up!" Ethel retorted. "I expect Oscar to get lost in the standing grass one of these days." This was a thinly veiled reference to the fact that Oscar was not a tall man. Oscar was five feet two; Ethel was five feet eight.

But it was the question of grass on the garden path that brought the two old lovebirds to the verbal equivalent of blows. "Ethel" Oscar said in a quietly admonitory voice. "I wish you wouldn't walk in the same tracks every time you go to the garden. You are wearing out my grass. You could walk..."

Oscar aimed to say more. In fact he aimed to tell Ethel how she could vary her route so that there would be less wear and tear on the grass. But she interrupted the flow of admonition.

"Your grass! Your grass! I need a path to the garden and I will walk in the same tracks until I get a path and then I..."

"But you're killing the grass!"

"So what's a little strip out of four acres of grass? Don't you have enough grass to pet and pamper without that little strip? Do you have to cover the whole earth with your sacred grass?"

And that's the way the garden path came to be.

But Oscar was not one to give up easily. He was not a man who backs away from a little marital confrontation. Not at all. While Ethel was setting her tomato plants across the South side of the garden Oscar scattered grass seeds on the worn area, then put the sprinkler on it in the hope that the seeds would germinate quickly and repair the damage done by Ethel's constant trudging on his grass.

Ethel encountered the sprinkler as it was getting dark under the trees; she was furious. She spoke to Oscar in her most controlled tones. "Oscar, I will not have my good garden shoes ruined by traipsing through the water in order to reach the house." Then she noticed the mud on the carpet. "And I see that you have preceded me. Now we will have grass sprouting in the carpet." Oscar disconnected the sprinkler, the ground dried out, and Ethel walked back and forth on the path, dry shed. Like the children of Israel crossing the Red Sea.

Oscar fumed and planned a new strategy. He covered the newly planted seeds with wheat straw. The straw cushioned Ethel's tramping, the seeds would sprout and be protected by the layer of straw, and Ethel could not complain about mud, either on her shoes or on the carpet, because the straw would take care of that problem. Oscar stood hack to wait and watch.

It didn't work. Ethel had bought a powerful leaf blower for keeping Oscar' leaves off her lettuce bed and she started it up and dragged it down the garden path with the result that all the wheat straw was blown away. As she was bringing her Troy Bilt garden tiller to the tool shed she accidentally let the tines touch down and they dug out the last clump of original grass on the path. This time it was Oscar's turn to be furious.

"Dammit all Ethel! Do you HAVE to crank that damn tiller while you're on the path?" Ethel did not hear all of what he was saying because of the loud noise the tiller was making. Besides, just as she passed under the dogwood tree the tines struck a root near the surface and the Troy Bilt Pony ran away with her.

"Now see what you made me do, Oscar!" she cried. "Why can't you attend to your own business for a change?"

The next day a large truck arrived bearing the lettering Green Grow Sod Company on its sides. Ethel was not in her garden when the grass sod was unloaded. It was the day of the Happy Valley Garden Club meeting and Elsie Farnsworth was entertaining the group. Sandwiches of lettuce, green onions and asparagus tips were served outdoors near Elsie's garden and the program featured organic gardening; a good time was had by all. When Ethel returned home a continuous green swath was stretched from the back door step to the very edge of her butter beans on the southwest tip of her garden. Ethel observed Oscar's latest work of art in absolute silence.

On that same day at eight o'clock in the evening Oscar received a telegram notifying him of the death of his Aunt Matilda in Waukegan. Oscar was appointed in Aunt Matilda's will as executor of her estate and it was necessary for him to go to Waukegan to handle this business which turned out to be very much involved with numerous brothers, sisters and cousins and numberless nephews and nieces who had to be searched out and satisfied. As a result of this Oscar was away from home for five days in which time Ethel remained busy in her garden.

Oscar was so busy with the matters of the will of his Aunt Matilda that he hardly had time to think of his grass which had grown to more than six inches in his absence and when he returned he saw that the long curving, dipping and rising green strip was still in place but beside it the old established grass was already beginning to show the unmistakable signs of wear which told him that Ethel had begun to beat a new path beside the old.

To Bury A Baptist

Father Corcoran came to the little southwest Georgia town of Good Hope just as Spring was running out and Summer was barging in. The waters of time and circumstance were flowing swiftly for James Sylvester Corcoran. He had graduated from the Theological Seminary; he had been ordained to the Episcopal priesthood; he had married Sheila Rowlett; and he had been assigned by the Bishop, Joseph Lattimer, to his first charge in rapid fire succession.

He arrived at Saint John of the Fields in a state of elation and uncertainty about just what to do next. He soon found out that there was not much for him to do. There were twenty seven communicants of Saint John of the Fields in Good Hope Georgia. Most of what there was to do in Good Hope was already being done by the Baptists of Good Hope.

To be truthful, the Methodists did have a little toe hold in Good Hope. But they were not doing anything big. No big building program. No big promotional campaign. No big Evangelistic Rally. The Baptists were doing all these things.

The Baptists were building a new and enlarged- and enriched-sanctuary. The Baptists were raising unprecedented sums of money for the Cooperative Program. The Baptists were conducting a Billy Graham type revival and raking in the new members by the netfull. The Baptists...the Baptists...There was no end to what the Baptists were doing in Good Hope. And nothing left for any body else to do. Not even for the Methodists, let alone the twenty seven Episcopalians at Saint John of the Fields.

No Methodist was President of the only bank in Good Hope. No Episcopalian either. A Baptist was. No Methodist was President of the Chamber of Commerce. Or Mayor of the town.

Or Superintendent of Schools. No Episcopalian was either. All these offices were held by Baptists. Methodists and a scattering of Episcopalians were Vice Presidents. Second echelon people.

And of course there were the Holiness people who held no positions of prestige or influence at all in Good Hope. Brother Stickleman the preacher at the Holiness Church had his hands full just holding what he had and when he was asked how his little flock was faring, said "As fast as I get them into the fold they just jump right out again."

And Father Corcoran had been sent by Bishop Lattimer to be the rector of the little twenty-seven member Saint John of the Fields Episcopal Church. He and his wife Sheila brought that number to twenty nine. But Father Corcoran was undaunted. Was he not a graduate of the Theological Seminary where all sacred wisdom is taught? Was he not a priest of the Episcopal Church wherein all truth is lodged? And a goodly portion of God's Grace as well? And was he not the happy Bridegroom who goeth forth rejoicing? And had he not been SENT by the Bishop to Good Hope to build up the Church and to confirm the members thereof in the Faith?

Now all he had to do was go out and learn from the Baptists and maybe a little from the Methodists, and some others, how to do it. So on the second day after his arrival in town he adjusted his clerical collar and very self consciously sallied forth into the field to do battle for the Lord, for the Bishop, and for Saint John. It was necessary, of course, that he get acquainted with his fellow laborers in the vineyard, namely Doctor Peter Hawke, the pastor of the First Baptist Church; the Reverend Ellwood Hopkins, minister of the Good Hope United Methodist Church; and Brother Eli Stickleman the Holiness preacher.

Father Corcoran approached the imposing Gothic structure which was the First Baptist Church of Good Hope, located, quite appropriately on Church Street and occupying, with the new steepled structure rising beside the old, half the block between Oak and maple Streets. Four private dwellings remained on the block but they appeared doomed. Already they exhibited the signs of neglect and disrepair which tell the world that their occupants have given up hope of maintaining their lease.

"Their future is the object of prayer, no doubt," Jim Corcoran mused. He was thinking of the President of his Seminary who was reputed to have prayed several residents out of their houses in the path of the Seminary's expansion. He paused for a moment, studying the sign which read First Baptist Church of Good Hope

Peter Hawke, Ph.D. Minister

Renew Good Hope All you who Enter Here

He walked in at the door marked Church Office. Three secretaries were busily transacting Baptist business. One, a brunette in her mid thirties, was talking animatedly on the telephone. A blonde girl with the bloom of youth on her handsome features, was studiously consulting the files. An older woman who looked up from a computer screen and .turned an inquiring smile on the visitor, said "May I help you?" She was thinking Now who sent you?

"Yes," the visitor replied. "I'm Father Corcoran. Is Doctor Hawke in?"

The matronly woman pressed an intercom button and spoke in a barely audible voice. "A Catholic priest here to see you."

"Send him in." Peter Hawke laid the travel folders he was studying on his desk and rose to meet his visitor.

"Jim Corcoran," the priest said. "Episcopal. Saint John's"

"Elsie scared me half out of my wits there. I'm Peter Hawke. I'm glad to meet you. Welcome to Good Hope. So you're not really an emissary of the Pope come to see what the Baptists are up to now?"

"Afraid not, but I'd still like to know what you Baptists are doing. Whatever it is you must be doing it right." The visiting priest sat down and prepared to be told what the Baptists were doing right.

"Well right now I'm preparing for a trip to the Holy Land." Peter Hawke slapped the travel folders on his desk. "I leave next week. Already I'm beginning to suspect that somebody here wants to get me out of town so I'll quit meddling in the building program."

When Jim Corcoran was leaving, Peter Hawke walked him to the door and made a point of saying in the presence of the three secretaries "Glad to have you on board the good ship Hope to help with the lost souls, Father Corcoran. Soon as you get settled in bring your wife around to meet Nancy and the kids. We still had two the last time I was home. You got any?"

"Not yet. I've only been married three weeks."

When he had gone the matronly secretary rolled her eyes at Peter Hawke. "A Catholic priest with a wife? I thought they weren't allowed to marry."

"Only those of the Anglican persuasion," he replied teasing the church secretary. "Special dispensation by King Henry the Eighth."

"I declare Doctor Hawke, I can never tell when you are serious and when you are joking." She made a despairing gesture.

"Always serious. Even when I'm joking."

"He's a serious joker," the girl studying the files said when Peter Hawke's door closed behind him.

Jim Corcoran's next stop was at the Methodist Church. It was locked and there was no sign indicating a Church Office. He spied what appeared to be the Methodist parsonage next door and investigation proved his hunch to be right. The Reverend Hopkins was home. His church office was there too. It was a book and magazine and church periodical cluttered study just off the front parlor which was doing double duty as a play area for the preacher's youngest, a four year old boy named Benjie, a rather precocious lad who stared at the priest with wide grey eyes, ran to his father, hugged his knees and said "Daddy, it's the Bishop. Hold me."

Ellwood Hopkins held Benjie on his knee while he got acquainted with the Episcopal rector. After about ten minutes Benjie's mother came and enticed him away with a promise of cookies. Her name was Sarah and her face was flushed, her hair was disorderly and she smiled beautifully. "It's wash day," she said. "And I'm cooking lunch. You're invited to stay and eat with us in about thirty minutes."

Father Corcoran was tempted but decided he had better not disturb the matrimonial waters so recently entered. "Sheila's expecting me to sample her latest attempt and tell her if it's good. I hope the Lord is merciful to liars who serve a higher cause in the interest of domestic bliss."

Within the next fifteen minutes he learned that Ellwood Hopkins and his family were going on their annual vacation, starting next week, that they would be gone for two or three weeks, that they would spend this vacation at a Youth Retreat where Ellwood would be the Counselor in Waiting. Ellwood explained that he would be waiting for whatever might happen when half a hundred teen age boys and girls were separated from their parents three hundred miles from home.

"If you see any stray Methodists wandering about Good Hope and looking as if they are about to fall into sin, take them in and administer large doses of ecclesiastical concern. It can't hurt them and I'll be grateful. Maybe my Bishop will even bless your Bishop for it."

On his way home Father Corcoran encountered a tall rangy man with reddish hair to match his reddish face. "I'm Brother Stickleman," the man said. "I reckon you are the new man of God in town."

In the ensuing conversation Brother Stickleman made the observation on the sheep of his flock which has already been noted. He also let the priest know that he was a working man and he was working for the next few weeks on a job about forty miles away. "They say Jesus was a carpenter till he started preaching. I started preachin' and have been carpenterin' ever since to make a livin'." He extended a work callused hand to Jim Corcoran as he made his departure.

Three days after Peter Hawke left for the Holy Land and Ellwood Hopkins left for Camp Leatherwood, Martin Curry died. Martin Curry was the biggest Baptist in Good Hope.

Martin Curry was Chairman of the Deacons of First Baptist Church. He was President of the only bank in Good Hope. Chairman of the local School Board. Very wealthy. And the recognized head of one of the leading families in town . His oldest son Malcomn, a lawyer, came to the young Episcopal priest and explained the situation. "Our minister, Doctor Hawke, has gone to the Holy Land on a guided tour; it would be very inconvenient to ask him to come back for my father's funeral. The Methodist minister is away too and is mixing vacation with church related duties involving a large group of young people. My family has agreed that I should ask you to conduct funeral services for my father." Malcomn Curry did not mention Brother Stickleman who was carpentering forty miles from Good Hope and trying to recapture the sheep who kept escaping from his fold.

Father Corcoran was taken by surprise and he did not know what to say, so he said he would consult his Bishop since he had no experience of this sort of thing.

He called Bishop Lattimer and detailed the situation very much as Malcomn Curry had put it to him. Then he asked if the Bishop would give his blessing to his performance of this sad and extraordinary service for the Baptist Martin Curry of Good Hope.

"By all means my son," Bishop Joseph Lattimer replied. "Bury all the Baptists you can in Good Hope."

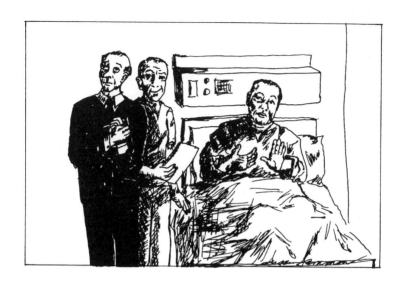

The Bottom Line

"Chaplain Steele! You're just the man I'm looking for." The doctor, still wearing his surgical greens, was hurrying towards the nurses' station but he stopped in mid flight and whirled about to face the hospital chaplain. "This man Roberts-Combs Roberts- from the mountains. I wish you would look in on him and let me know what you think."

"I see." The chaplain did not see at all what Doctor Nathan Sullivan was getting at. "What is it you want me to look for in Combs Robert."

"Not the bullet." The doctor chuckled at his own wit but he had not yet shed any light on the chaplain's path. "I got it. He's resting well. Don't expect any complications. Missed his spine by more than an inch. But it's all a mystery. How he got himself shot."

"It sounds interesting," the chaplain conceded, and waited.

"Well, he was shot and you know how these mountain people are. Always feuding over something. Shooting somebody whose grandpappy shot his grandpappy."

"I read something about the Hatfields and McCoys, but I'm afraid that doesn't make me an expert on feuding in the mountains."

"Well, this man's been shot and I'm curious. I wish you'd try to get at the bottom of it."

Chaplain Harvey Steele made a note to see Combs Roberts who had been shot. He stuffed the note inside his jacket pocket.

Inside his head he formed the words: "I have twenty two Pre-Ops to see before they are hauled away on rubber tired carts to the operating rooms tomorrow and Nate Sullivan wants me to get to the bottom of a mystery shooting in the mountains."

A Pre-Op is a person who knows he is going to surgery and pretends not to be concerned at all about it because he has the utmost confidence in his medical doctor's skill, but in actuality he is scared stiff and all atremble inside because of what might happen. to him if something does go wrong. Of course those things only happen to one in a zillion but when a fellow is checked into the hospital, stripped of his clothes, covered with a split tail fig leaf gown, and ordered to pee in a bottle, then he is sure that he is the one that Fate has singled out for disaster.

And the chaplain must present himself to each one of those trembling Pre-Ops, all twenty two of them in Chaplain Steele's case, and reassure each one of them that if the worst does happen he will be standing there holding his hand, offering all the benefits of clergy to his anxious family, and breathing a prayer that God will enter into the equation at the moment of greatest peril to succor the needy when all human efforts fail.

Chaplain Steele was about half way through the Pre-Ops list when Brother Raspberry, the pastor of the Mount Pisgah Baptist Church stopped him in the stairwell between the first and second floors of the hospital.

Brother Raspberry wanted to tell Chaplain Steele about one of his church members who was in the hospital for observation and Brother Raspberry indicated that this church member would bear observation by the chaplain as well as by the medical team because he was one of the heaviest givers in his church and very faithful in attendance at all church functions.

The church member under observation had made a sizable contribution to the hospital's building fund and this alone made him worthy of observation.

Brother Raspberry had a very inspiring service on the Sunday past with three professions of faith and two rededications all of which had greatly elevated Brother Raspberry's spirits and he was moved to tell the chaplain about it. And he did.

Returning to his office to find out what room the man shot in the mountains, one Combs Roberts, was resting in, Doctor Sullivan having failed to mention that little detail, the chaplain arrived to find that it was a mistake to go back by the office. The telephone on his desk was ringing insistently and a visitor, a complete stranger to the chaplain but a man who appeared to be quite at home in the chaplain's office, was waiting for him to return from his Pre-Op rounds.

The telephone call was urgent; the ringing could not be ignored. And when he answered he learned that the caller was Genevieve Hawley who was President of the Women's Auxiliary.

The WA was holding its monthly meeting in the chapel on next Tuesday and Mrs. Hawley wanted Chaplain Steele to address the WA on the subject of the ways in which the WA members could be helpful in carrying out his ministry to the hospital patients and their families, and Mrs. Hawley told Chaplain Steele six or seven things that she thought he might say to the WA, all six or seven items being helpful things they could do to help him in his ministry.

The visitor sitting on the uncomfortable imitation leather chair facing the chaplain's desk did not seem to be bothered at all by the telephone call. In fact, he seemed mildly interested and even nodded his assent when Chaplain Steele agreed to speak to the WA on the topic which Genevieve Hawley had suggested.

When the telephone conversation had ended Chaplain Steele turned to his visitor and learned that his name was Jerry Adkins and that he was a born again Christian who would welcome any and every opportunity to witness for his Lord, especially to people who are sick and in great need of such comfort, that being the condition of all who are to be found in the Memorial Baptist Hospital.

Jerry also informed the chaplain that he was in need of employment and that he was willing to work either as an orderly helping with patients in the hospital, or as a maintenance man keeping the place in good repair, whichever of the two positions would afford the greater opportunity for him to witness.

Chaplain Steele suggested that Jerry Adkins see the Maintenance Supervisor who might find a place for him keeping the lawns and parking lots clean and presentable. Jerry Adkins seemed a bit disappointed that he would not have as many opportunities to witness on the lawn and parking lot as he had hoped for in the rooms and corridors, but he thought there might be some in the form of people going to and from the parking lot and needing a word of direction as to how to find the Lord.

Chaplain Steele still had ten Pre-Op patients to see but it was getting late and Doctor Sullivan's Mystery Man of the Mountains kept nagging at his mind.

"I may as well try to get to the bottom of this thing and get it over with," he said to himself, feeling guilty about the ten Pre-Ops who might have to face the terrors of surgery without benefit of clergy. He consulted the Registry and learned that Combs Roberts was in Room 186 and there he found him propped up in bed and eating his supper from a tray. Wishing to ease into the subject in an unobtrusive manner, the chaplain introduced himself and said "Tell me about yourself. Where you live. What you do. How you came to be here in Memorial Baptist Hospital."

Combs Roberts was a tall thin man in his middle thirties with dark tangled hair, three days of stubble on his face which was characterized by a pallor which indicated that he did not spend his days in bright sunshine. Loss of blood might be a factor too but Chaplain Steele did not want to rush into that matter.

Combs Roberts' jaws moved rhythmically as he chewed his Salisbury steak thoroughly. This activity gave him time to thoroughly examine the chaplain's three pronged question and prepare an answer that would not divulge any damaging information. When he had swallowed the food and taken a sip of coffee he addressed the first part of the question.

"I live up on Brushy Mountain in Perry County," Combs Roberts said. "You know where Huggins Creek runs alongside the state road just before you git to the county line?"

Chaplain Steele was not intimately acquainted with the geography of Perry County although he remembered having driven to Hazard once, but he was willing to settle for Combs Roberts' description of the area where he lived, so he moved on to the second part of the question which Combs Roberts seemed to have forgotten.

"What kind of work are you doing up there on Huggins Creek, Mister Roberts?"

"Oh I just live on Huggins Creek. I'm a coal miner. I work in Mine Number Seven over the county line in Letcher. You know where Lilley Woods is? And Kingdom Come?"

Chaplain Steele had been to the Lilley Cornett Woods and was greatly impressed by the virgin forest there, as well as disturbed by rumors that the coal interests were eager to dig up the minerals underneath the roots of those giant trees that had escaped the axes and saws of the timber men.

He had visited the Kingdom Come School too. Not that he

had any particular business there, but the name intrigued him. He still had no idea where Mine Number Seven was but it was irrelevant to his main mission which was to get to the bottom of the mystery. And, since he viewed his role in a broader light than Doctor Sullivan had implied by his request, to help Combs Roberts to cope with whatever animosities, hostilities or enmities might lie at the root of the mystery of his shooting.

"Doctor Sullivan tells me you were shot," the chaplain said coming to grips with the mystery. "How did that happen?"

Combs Roberts was surprisingly forthcoming in his response. "My neighbor shot me. Fellow lives down the road a piece from me. He shot me."

"Had you and your neighbor been having some trouble?" The chaplain discounted the idea of a feud, but still...

"Not really. Fact is, I hardly knowed the man. Never more'n spoke to 'im in passin'."

The chaplain waited with an inquiring expression that said "Yes, go on."

"I knowed his wife real well. Real well."

Returning to his office Chaplain Steele encountered Doctor Sullivan whose countenance bore an inquiring expression.

"Yes, Doctor," the chaplain said. "I think I got to the bottom of it. But then again, maybe not. You know these mountain people are deep."

Henry Buchanan, the Georgia-bred story teller, is an adopted son of Kentucky. A professional marriage counselor and hospital chaplain, he has had many articles published in magazines and newspapers. Now he is writing fiction and short stories.

And The Goat Cried is the first of his stories to be published. He has promised Creative Arts many more to follow *The Goat* and since theology is his specialty we may expect him to reach from the very earthy to the nearly sublime.

❧ ❧ ❧

Susan Young Sammons of Murray, Kentucky illustrated the stories with her drawings.